BAD TIMES
AT BLAKE'S CANYON

Bad Times at Blake's Canyon

JOHNNY MACK BRIDE

A Black Horse Western

ROBERT HALE · LONDON

© Johnny Mack Bride 1993
First published in Great Britain 1993

ISBN 0 7090 5163 8

Robert Hale Limited
Clerkenwell House
Clerkenwell Green
London EC1R 0HT

Photoset in North Wales by
Derek Doyle & Associates, Mold, Clwyd.
Printed and bound in Great Britain by
WBC Ltd, Bridgend, Mid-Glamorgan.

ONE

The fire burned sluggishly, the wood being still green, and the sharp, bitter smoke quietly tormented them as they hunched around, red-eyed, their clay-streaked boots deep in the grey ashes. Cammil was spooning cornmeal mush into his mouth, a grey-wet smear of it plastering the beard around his lips and making him look like a great, dirty baby, cheerful but dangerous. Johnny Reb was gnawing the gristle off a bone, the remains of a piece of roasted horseflesh that he had been carrying with him for days. The rest were just squatting.

'Aw fuggit, Maxie! I gotta have more grub! Real vittles!' Cammil flung the empty tin pan violently away from him and rubbed his hand over his mouth, smacking his lips playfully. Even in hunger he wasn't angry, just cheerfully violent.

'Goddam fuggin' right!' Johnny Reb threw the bare bone after the discarded tin pan. 'Need fuggin' beef! Steak, an' taters an' bread an' stuff. Fuggin' bare bones ain't fittin' for a man.' He too grinned widely although he was cold and his belly empty. But then he always did grin – that excited, reckless *wrong* grin that wasn't related to humour but to madness. His real name was John Redbridges but that had become shortened to Johnny Red, and then, inevitably, to Johnny Reb.

Jack Holby stood up, the dried mud on his pants cracking with the movement. 'Yeah. An' I need a horse, Maxie. Gotta get one real soon. Must be a farm somewhere. But I gotta get one.' There was a faint threat underlying his remarks.

'Farm ain't no good to us,' Max Slievan growled. He remained in his squatting position, one arm round the shaking shoulders of his younger brother, Abe. 'Six men, hungry as all hell. An' we got other needs. Abe, here. Doctor or somethin'. We need a town.'

'Town?' They all looked at him. Slievan was the boss, but only marginally. He wasn't bigger or tougher than Holby, or crazier than Johnny Reb or more violent than Buff Cammil or more devious than Maccosino. He didn't know why he was the boss nor how long his power might hold. Maybe it was because there were two of them – him and Abe. And now Abe was sick, real sick. He sat, breathing hoarsely, with a damp, dirty blanket draped over his shivering shoulders, and his face was the colour of a wet gunny sack.

'Town might not be a good idea,' Tony Maccosino put in, absently poking the reluctant fire with a charred stick. 'Too many people in a town, even a small town. Always a chance that one or two will get away, put the law on us.'

Maccosino was the clever one, the thinker. He didn't look like the thinking type: at six foot two he was almost as tall as Holby but without Holby's fierce tension; a loose-limbed, open-mouthed, shambling man, he could strike with the lightning viciousness of an angry rattlesnake. He poked the fire again, meditatively, as though pushing his thoughts around in his mind. 'Farm would be a better idea,' he went on. 'Quiet farm, out of the way.' He looked at his associates, as though to impress on them the wisdom of his words. 'Quiet farms is always best – or a tradin' post, even. Get all you want there – grub, whisky, horses – an' there ain't likely to be too many people for us to handle.'

'Naw, an' there ain't likely to be a goddam fuggin' doctor!' Slievan spat out the words angrily, pushed beyond the risk of mutiny by a sudden violent spasm from the shivering Abe. 'We got a sick man here,' he harangued them. He rose to his feet, another lean, sullen six-footer, and glared around them. 'I know we gotta have grub. You ain't the only ones that's hungry. Yeah! An' you need a horse, I know!' he forestalled Holby. 'But we need other things too – clothes, ammunition, gun or two, maybe. Need goddam boots.'

'Git all them at a tradin' post,' mumbled Maccosino softly, still pushing the fire around.

'Yeah. But there's always men comin' an' goin' at tradin' posts – travellin' men, tradin' men, men that can shoot, an' fight.'

'Always men comin' an' goin' in towns,' insisted Maccosino gently, still poking.

'Maybe ... maybe,' Slievan stalled, 'but they ain't always so ... capable. They're storekeepers, men with families. Easier pickin's. 'Sides, we don't know where any tradin' post is at.'

'You know where there's a town?' Buff Cammil stood up, scratching himself and grinning in anticipation.

'Yeah, I reckon.' Slievan was quick to cash in on the interest. 'This trail's showin' signs of light traffic. I figger it's goin' somewhere soon. You'll get all you want there. An' Abe here'll get treatment. Aw, Jesus!' he swore as his brother Abe fell over in a paroxysm of coughing. 'Help me with him, Holby. Help me get him on his horse. Hold on now, Abe, son! You be awright. Gonna git you a fuggin' doctor. Aw, give us a fuggin' hand for Chrissakes willya, Holby!'

Holby leaned down and grabbed the sick man by an arm and leg. 'Awright,' he grinned sourly. 'Long as you know I'm gittin' me a horse. From your town or somewheres else.' He paused for a moment, careless of the groaning man they held between them. 'Come to think,' he thought aloud, 'your town's probably best. I got more choice of mounts there. 'Sides,' he grinned lewdly, 'I got other needs too.'

They carried the sick man over to the horses and heaved him into his saddle where he slumped, shivering and coughing, holding on to the saddle horn with both hands. 'Jus' hold on, Abe, son,' Slievan urged him, his tone one of genuine concern. 'We'll git you into a bed real soon. Git you a fuggin' doctor. You'll be awright.'

They began to mount. Holby's horse was in a bad way. A second-rate animal to begin with, it had been reduced to near foundering by merciless hard riding and total neglect. Its hoofs were split and its mouth bleeding, while great sores showed in front of and behind the saddle, suggesting what lay underneath. Holby jerked violently at the reins and kicked it casually in the belly as it sidled fearfully away from him.

Maccosino looked down on him from his own mount. 'You don' deserve a decent horse,' he said. 'Don't never look after him right. When I take a horse I take a good one. An' I look after him, keep him in good shape.'

'Your ass, Mako!' rejoined Holby contemptuously. 'This bastard warn't no good to start with.'

'Then you shouldn' a took him. I wouldn' never take a poor animal. You don' see me ridin' no crowbaits.'

'Aw, quit yappin' willya, Mako?' Holby heaved his bulk into the saddle. 'When you took that horse you had time, an' you had a choice. You weren't afoot — an' the goddam owner warn't shootin' at you.' He spurred the sick animal with casual brutality and took after the others in a weak, faltering canter.

They had to ride slowly because of Abe but two hours of travelling brought them to the mouth of the canyon.

'There's a place in there all right,' mumbled Mako in his slack, open-mouthed way. 'Tracks lead right on in. Few wheel tracks, some shod horses. Not many though. Must be a small place.'

'How we gonna do it, Maxie?' Buff Cammil, the weakest minded and therefore the most easily led, looked towards his boss, his fat, childish face showing interest and obedience.

'Shit!' Holby looked at Cammil, the insolent blue eyes in the big craggy face gleaming with contempt. 'Jus' fuggin' goin' in, that's how.' He stabbed his trembling mount with his spurs, causing it to plunge shakily forward.

A big man, Holby, and very, very strong. Six feet four and as thick as a tree, there wasn't an ounce of spare flesh on him. His trunk was like the barrel of a steam locomotive, his arms and legs like terrible lean pistons. An almost completely physical man. Some men think first and act afterwards; others think and act simultaneously; others act first and then reflect on the consequences. Holby was none of these types: Holby simply acted; there *was* no thought, before or after – or rather, action *was* thought, the only kind of consciousness he had.

And he was terribly strong. At the age of twenty-two, working as a cowboy and wrestling a steer, he had broken the animal's neck in a fit of annoyance. Thereafter he had performed the feat regularly, from time to time, to demonstrate his strength and to know that he could do it. Indeed, he owed his present way of life to the fact that when the foreman had sacked him for this expensive behaviour he had become angry and, being angry, he had put a head lock on the foreman, and, knowing that he could break his neck, had naturally done so. He had been on the run ever since.

'Hold on a goddamn minute!' Slievan called harshly. He wasn't afraid of Holby. Max Slievan wasn't afraid of anybody, but he didn't want mutiny, not now, with Abe real sick. They needed every man if they were to take and hold this small town. 'You want the bastards to come at you with guns?' he shouted. 'Coupla dozen of 'em? You gonna take on a small fuggin' army of 'em?'

'Why would they go for their guns?' Holby let his faltering mount stop. He stared back insolently. 'They'll think we're jus' passin' riders. Saddle tramps.'

'Naw, Maxie's right,' grinned Johnny Reb. 'They take one look at us an' run to get their guns. Happens every time. Unless they're too scared.' He laughed in puzzled amusement. 'Mus' be some-thing' about us, heh?'

'Another thing,' Slievan went on, taking advantage of the pause, 'we don't want nobody gittin' away, goin' for the law. You, Johnny,' he nodded to Redbridges. 'You stay here. Stay mounted. Some of these little canyons only got one way in – folks go in and out the same way. Maybe this one's like that. You wait here. Anybody comes hightailin' it this way you make sure he don't go noplace. When we're settled we'll send for ya.'

Johnny Reb touched the brim of his hat in a grinning mock salute.

'But Max.' It was the sick man who spoke. He

looked up at his brother, his long, greasy hair hanging damply to his shoulders. His face showed exhaustion, worry, even the beginnings of fear. 'What if they fight back? What if there's too many of 'em? What if ...?' He broke down again in another spasm of coughing.

'Get the kids,' Maccosino countered. 'That always works. Every time.'

'Yeah.' Slievan nodded approvingly. 'Good man, Mako.' He turned to Cammil. 'Buff? When we ride in, you go round back of the town. See if there's another way out. If there is, wait there and keep it shut, like Johnny at this end. Holby, you stick with me an' Mako here. You'll git your horse, if you'll jus' hang on a little while.'

Holby shrugged. 'Okay. I don' mind – long as I get my way.' His tone was one of sincere reasonableness. 'You know me: I don't mind workin', don't mind fightin', don't mind nothin' – long as I get my way.'

'Okay,' grunted Slievan. 'Let's go.'

TWO

The people of Blake's Canyon took one look at them and realized that life had suddenly taken one of those terrible, unpredictable swerves, and that things had somehow gone badly wrong.

There were not many people about. Lou Gans was in his store, as usual, endlessly checking lists, estimating profits, devising little swindles; Edie Stacey, his assistant, was shrewdly sweet-talking customers and occasionally casting calculating glances at Lou where he worked with paper and pencil between the shelves; Joe Gregory was at his forge, absently shaping a horseshoe on the anvil but really thinking about his idea for some kind of fireplace arrangement that would make cooking quicker and easier for the womenfolk; Jim Moller was in the livery stable, checking sick horses and wondering whether the owner of the stable would ever sell to him.

None of these people detected any change in things, but the few who were on the street took one look at the mud-caked horses, the bristling clutter of weapons, the men themselves and the clothes that grew on them like fungus and they knew that something alien and perilous had happened upon them.

Slievan and Mako came first, riding on each side of Abe and supporting him in his saddle. Holby trailed several yards behind, his mount trembling visibly in the legs. The people watched, their wonder turning to dread, and waited.

'Got a doctor in this town?' Slievan spoke from the saddle.

The people were slow to react, frightened by something in the voice.

'You got a doctor, goddamit!' Slievan rasped, urged on by a spasm of coughing from the sick man. 'Any kinda medical man? Somebody, for Chrissakes! We got a sick man here.' Mako quietly dismounted.

Isaac Stone spoke. Isaac, at fifty, was one of the older men and one of the kind that took responsibility. 'Why no,' he faltered. 'I mean … no … that is … no doctor. We got Ben Partlin, but he. …' He stopped, wishing that he hadn't said those words.

'You got any kinda fuggin' medical man?' Slievan swung down from the saddle, his voice becoming an angry snarl. 'Nurse or somethin', for Chrissakes. Aw Jesus!' he swore as Abe slumped from his saddle to the ground, one foot caught in a stirrup. 'Give us a fuggin' han' here willya!'

The little crowd had grown to a dozen people. They stared, fascinated. Normally, they would have rushed to help a sick man, but now … they couldn't, somehow. Just couldn't.

'Ya dumb bastards! Ya fuggin' deaf?' Slievan roared. 'Get your medical man here!'

There was a moment's distraction. On the edge of the crowd old Dan Pender experienced an overwhelming panic: in a moment of insight he saw that these men could not be appeased and he realized simultaneously that not one of the townspeople was armed. He thought of the rifle that he had resting above his fireplace at home and broke away in a panicky arthritic scrabble to try to reach his cabin.

Holby, coming easily up from behind, saw him, swept forward in a swift rush and had him instantly in a vice-like head lock.

The old man stopped absolutely, all movement ceasing with the pain and only muffled, strangulated appeals coming out from the knot of arms and head. The crowd stared, shocked, and afraid. Holby grinned, enjoying his audience. He looked around the white faces and saw that they were looking at him – him, Jack Holby! He savoured the moment then gave a vicious, expert twist. There was an audible crack. Holby held his position for a moment, for effect, then let go and stepped back, his trick performed. The old man crumpled to the ground and lay motionless, a lifeless bundle of bones and old clothes.

The edges of the crowd trembled, as though the people might scatter in panic, but there was a scuffle of movement and Mako's voice rang out. 'Hold it! Hold it! Don' move or I'll blow her fuggin' head off!'

He shoved forward into plainer view. He held a thirteen-year-old girl by the hair and he had a big .44 pistol rammed against her ear.

'Yeah!' Slievan dropped the sick Abe, lunged forward and grabbed a shock-headed boy of about eleven. 'Don't none of ya move – else he gits it too.' He had a Colt out and he shoved it under the boy's jaw, forcing the head upwards and back. Loud, gasping wails trailed out from the two youngsters and there was a furious eruption of movement in the crowd as a man surged forward.

'You bastards! Take your goddam hands off my. ...'

There was a fearful thud as Holby hit him straight between the eyes with a fist like a mallet. The man staggered, his hands to his face, and Holby followed up. He hit him again, and again, measured, calculated blows that sounded like a hammer hitting rock. The man reeled helplessly under the blows for a few seconds then crashed to the ground. 'Anybody else want to try?' shouted Holby, the blue eyes glaring through the thick forelock of hair that hung over the craggy brow.

The small crowd was growing. People were running towards the scene from the surrounding cabins and buildings. They slowed down and stopped when they saw the situation.

'Now,' rasped Slievan, sure of himself, 'where's this doctor fella ... this Ben somebody?'

Some people at the back turned their heads. A little balding, fifty-year-old man tried to retreat, to shrink away into nothing. 'I ain't no doctor,' he protested, his hands held out defensively, his voice plainly fearful. 'Don' know nothin' 'bout medicine. Jus' an ordinary ...'

'Come here, goddam you!' snarled Slievan. The little man came forward, cringing.

'You do the nursin' aroun' here, huh?'

Ben Partlin tried to speak but no words came out.

Slievan looked at a woman in the front of the crowd. 'This your medical man?'

There was the briefest of nods, a bare, terrified twitch of the chin.

Slievan glared at the little man. 'Okay. We got a patient for you. Where do ya live?'

'But I don' know nothin' about medicine!' The words tumbled out of Ben Partlin now. 'Jus' do what anybody would. Anybody else can do ...'

'Shuddup!' Slievan roared. He shoved the pistol hard up under the boy's chin, forcing the head back and making the boy cry out. 'You'll do what I tell ya, or there'll be brains flyin' aroun' in the air – an' not jus' his. Now, you, little bald fella, you're the medical man. You got the job – an' you better do it real good, else you won' be walkin' aroun' no more. You an' you,' he indicated two men in the front rank, 'pick up our frien' here,' he nodded to where Abe lay on the ground, among the feet of the horses, 'an' bring him along. Holby?'

Holby looked around. 'Yeah?'

'Grab that little medicine fella an' make him show you where he lives. We'll use his house for Abe. Okay, let's go.'

Still holding the two squalling youngsters they moved along the street. Holby led the way, dragging Ben Partlin by the collar. The crowd remained frozen where they were then, after a stunned couple of minutes, began to look at each other and try to communicate. Half a dozen men and women sank to their knees around old Dan Pender and began to examine the body wonderingly. The man Holby had felled dragged himself to his feet, his head bloody in his hands. One or two men drifted, in a disoriented, bewildered manner, after the gang.

Fifteen minutes later Buff Cammil rode in and five minutes after that Slievan came out of a log-and-sod house and faced the few men hanging around. He had his Colt in his hand.

'Hey! C'mere!' he called, motioning with his pistol, and those nearby edged apprehensively closer. 'Now listen,' he told them. 'We're gonna be here a while. Don't know how long. Man needs treatment, an' we ain't leavin' till he's better. Now you're gonna co-operate: if ya don't, there'll be some dead kids lyin' aroun' – an' some mammies an' daddies as well. Don' think we won't do it, 'cause we will.' He paused to let that fact sink in. 'So don't none of you try to escape. There ain't no back way out of here, I know. An' I'm puttin' a man in the livery stable, where he can watch the only way in an' out. It'll be watched night an' day.

'Now I'm gonna send two men to bring in every gun you've got in this town.' He looked across the street to where Holby stood with Mako. 'There ain't no more'n fifteen or twenty cabins in the goddam place. That way there won't be no temptation put in nobody's way.'

He motioned at them again with his pistol. 'Now listen good: you go along with us an' you'll be awright. Won't nobody get hurt much. We jus' want treatment for Abe.' He spoke as if the people knew his brother personally. 'Oh, an' a horse or two ... little ammunition, maybe ... an' some goddam clothes. An' we gotta be fed. Ain't et right for months.

'Now we're gonna be stayin' here, in this shack – me, an' Abe an' Johnny – along with Ben Partlin. An' I'm puttin' a man in the forge an' a man in the store, along with the man in the livery stable – they'll be there all the time. An' they gotta be fed – an' good chow, ya hear? Best you've got. Work it out amongst ya who does the feedin' an' when, but you better see that it's done, 'cause if it ain't they'll come lookin' for it an' you won't like that, I promise you.

'Right,' he nodded in their direction. 'That's it. Aside for that you can jus' live like ordinary, way you usually do. I'll let ya know if there's anythin' else. G'wan now, an' tell the rest.'

He motioned them away with his pistol and beckoned across to Holby. 'Holby,' he said, watching the retreating backs of the townsmen, 'you an' Mako go roun' the cabins – store too, every place – an' get every gun they got. Make sure you git ever' one. Take a kid with you, with a gun in his ear. Those bastards will co-operate awright.

They're shit scared. Bring the guns back here. Then you go in the store, an' stay there. Mako goes in the forge.'

'The store for Chrissakes? What the hell for? I got better things to do.' The fierce blue eyes blazed with mutinous resentment.

'Look, I know what I'm doin',' Slievan interrupted him. 'I don't figure them bastards'll make any trouble, but there's a lot of them. Ya can't never be sure. Maybe some brave bastard among them'll want to be a hero. Now besides their houses there's three main places – livery stable, store an' forge. I want a man in each place, 'cause them's the only places they can get stuff ... horses or some kinda weapons ... or, well, other kinds of stuff. I jus' wanna be sure, is all. 'Sides,' he went on, carefully sweetening the pill for Holby, 'that way you can get yourself stuff – boots, clothes, better gun, maybe. All kindsa stuff. You'll be awright.'

Holby snorted and moved off. Slievan went back inside the house. 'Cammil?' he said to the fat man, who sprawled in a chair in a corner. 'You ride out to the canyon mouth an' bring Johnny in. Tell him to come here. Then you go in the livery stable, an' stay there; see no bastard takes no horses. An' watch the trail, you can see it from there, see no bastard leaves.'

'Maybe somebody will ride in?' The fat face was creased in puzzlement.

'Yeah.' Slievan paused for thought. 'Don't think so though. Ain't many people on the trail this time of year ... winter not far away.' He paused again.

'If anybody does ride in: if it's one fella, blast him; if it's more'n one, run an' tell Holby – he'll be in the store. That where any riders will go first. Then come an' tell me an' Johnny. We'll get Mako.'

The fat man heaved himself up from his chair and waddled towards the door then stopped and looked around, his face screwed up in childish resentment. 'I gotta stay in the livery all the goddam fuggin time?'

'Yeah. All the goddam fuggin' time. You'll get fed. An' a little whisky, maybe. But don't get fuggin' drunk! I'll send Johnny down, time to time, give ya a break. Now get to it.'

In the adjoining room Abe, the sick man, stripped down to a filthy undervest and drawers, was lying almost motionless in the clean bed of Ben and Sarah Partlin. The wife stood beside her husband at the bedside clenching her hands, the knuckles white. The boy and girl hostages sat one in each corner, rigid with fear.

Slievan went in and, pistol still in hand, bent down over his brother. 'Awright, Abe.' He laid a hand on the shoulder of the prone form. 'Ya hear me? You're gonna be awright. We got you a medical man.' He turned to Ben Partlin. 'Now listen mister – Doc – you take care of Abe here. You get him well an' there'll be somethin' in it for you – money, horse maybe, other stuff – depends on what we got here, but we'll give ya …'

'But mister,' the little balding man broke in, desperate with fear, 'I ain't no medical man. Ain't even a horse doctor. All I did – we did—' He glanced fleetingly at his wife, 'was give some home remedies, kinda ... I don' know nothin' about real sickness. ... Don' even know what's wrong. ...'

'Shut your goddam mouth!' Slievan's shrill bellow was the noise of a man shutting out the truth he didn't want to hear. He shoved the muzzle of the Colt under Ben Partlin's chin, forcing his head back painfully. 'You've got the goddam job, mister. You're elected. You're the fuggin' medical man aroun' here. Now you get Abe well, or you'll wish to Jesus you hadn't never been born. An' her too!' He glared towards Ben's wife. 'An' them.' He indicated the two young hostages. 'An' half the bastards in this goddam town – men, women an' kids. We'll wipe out every fuggin' one of ya. Now get on with it!'

More than a hundred miles east of Blake's Canyon two men were making an early camp in a sheltered hollow, close to a little creek of good water. One lit a small fire and collected more wood while the other tended their horses.

The horse tender ran a hand over the back of his own mount, a big steeldust gelding. 'Yeah,' he mumbled, in a close-mouthed, lisping manner, 'it makes good sense to look after your animals.' He was a little over average height, lean, with slightly rounded shoulders, a narrow body and a stony face. His clothes were drab and functional, without any relieving colour. The rig he took from his horse was likewise devoid of any adornment. Altogether, in his clothes, gear, body language and general demeanour he gave an impression of dedicated joylessness. 'We coulda rode another five-ten mile,' he mumbled, half talking to himself, 'but we want to keep the horses fresh. 'Sides, there ain't no hurry.'

The man tending the blaze spoke. A softer man, a man carrying a little weight and with an unnecessary gold ear-ring in one ear. 'He could get away from us,' he said.

'Naw, he couldn't.' The reply was dry, matter of fact.

'I mean, he'll want to stay free. Be desperate to, you ask me. A desperate man'll do things an ordinary man won't … can't, even.'

'He's mine,' lisped the lean, colourless man.

The softer man looked at him with raised eyebrows but didn't speak any more.

Later, as they sat by the blaze, drinking coffee and belching from their stew and beans, the softer man spoke again. It was always he who began any conversations that they had.

'You still think he's headin' for that place?'

A curt nod.

'How can you be sure?'

'They always do.' There was a distant note of boredom in the voice. 'Like kids to their mammas.' A pause, then, 'He's got a wife there.'

'Aw, I see. But he might get there, pick her up and ride out, somewheres we don't know.'

The lean man gave a contemptuous snort. 'There ain't noplace he can go where I can't find him.'

THREE

The mule was tired, beat. He faced the fact at last, his legs sore and aching with drubbing at its skinny sides with his unspurred heels. He'd have to stop.

Goddamit! There was still an hour's travelling left, maybe an hour and a half. He swore in anger underlaid with fear and looked around him in the fading starlight, trying to find some place to hole up.

The mule slowed to a halt, recognizing the fact that he'd given in, and stood, head down, waiting, as mules do, for life to make the next move. He slid down from the bare, bony back and began to lead the animal off the trail, his naked feet slipping sorely in the lace-less boots.

It was still dark, goddamit! Where in hell was he going to find a place, safe place? Only thing he could do was get well of the trail, 'way to the side, and hope for some cover. And there was no water! Aw, Jesus!

It was a prayer more than a profanity, a sore, confused appeal to heaven. He stopped in his tracks, his whole body slumped and his face contorted with distress and despair; his shoulders shook and an anguished sob joined in the night air with the hoarse breathing of the mule. So he stood for perhaps twenty seconds, then he forced himself forward again, dragging the mule after him, because there was nothing else he could do.

He scraped his awkward way forward in the faint starlight. Across stony, dry washes, over bad-smelling, muddy creeks, stumbling frequently and blundering into scrub trees, cursing and whimpering he edged his way forward until he'd had more than enough. Then he tied the long-suffering mule to a dark bush in a stony hollow and started wondering about water.

He found some after some searching. 'Thick, and full of little animals,' he thought, as he scooped the soupy stuff to his mouth with his cupped hands while mosquitoes whined about his ears. But he swallowed it, because he had to.

Mule will have to get what feed it can, he thought, as he made his way back to the hollow. Mule can eat nearly any goddam thing. He was genuinely envious of that animal.

There was no food for him. He curled up on the stony ground, his empty belly tormenting him, and thought mouth-wateringly of how he might find some wild turnips the next day – or wild corn or wild onions – any goddam thing as long as he could eat it! He thought with longing of the bag of feed he'd got when he stole the mule. He'd always known you could eat horse-grain but he hadn't realized that in certain circumstances it could seem like the best food in the world. Sure, there was a lot of husk an' bran, but you could swallow that too after a while, an' it all helped to fill an empty belly and kept a man's bowels. ...

He suddenly stopped thinking, his mind taking a desperate avoidance swerve and becoming urgently filled with images of his wife, his stable, his two horses and the new foal – not a foal now: a two year old – and his cabin, wonderful, comfortable cabin, and food and coffee and warmth and a bed and safety.

He lay on the dark stony earth, shivering under the dirty cast-off coat that he'd found on the trail, the fetter-and-chain on his right wrist galling the raw black-and-red flesh, and he talked to himself, to reassure himself, to comfort himself.

The tethered mule tore at its bush with its leathery mouth, noisily chomping the bitter leaves and blowing its breath out in deep though wordless disgust. After a time a new sound could be heard accompanying the animal's browsing: a deep, sad, disturbing sound that would have frightened any human listener.

It was the sound of a man crying.

A deeply troubled impromptu meeting was being held half-in and half-out of old Dan Pender's place. The old man's body had been carried in and stretched out on his bed. His widow was now lying across the body, heaving and wailing with grief while two or three other women, tearful and dread-filled themselves, tried to comfort her.

On the porch and out into the street, a small crowd hung around, gabbling quietly among themselves.

'I know, I know, I know,' Isaac Stone insisted, trying to bring order into things, 'but don't do nothin' right away, not right now. There's nothin' we can do. Got to wait for the Lord's time.'

'Well, you might be waitin', Mister Stone, waitin' for the Lord. But they ain't got your girl in there,' protested Tom Morrow furiously. He was a slight, nondescript forty-five year old. 'I'm gonna get a gun from somewhere, or a weapon of some kind, and I'm gonna ...'

'No, don' do that Tom,' urged Doug Lambert. 'You seen what kinda men they are. They'd kill us all. Woundn' think nothin' of it. Isaac's right, we got to wait for the Lord's time.'

'They're right, Tom,' pleaded Louisa Morrow, wringing her hands in distress, her teeth biting her bottom lip. 'You go near them an' Thelma's likely to be the first to suffer. But, oh dear God!' She broke down, her face working convulsively. 'My girl in there with those ... those. ... Oh! God help us all!'

'Killed Old Dan Pender,' said a voice wonderingly. The speaker looked at anyone who would meet his eye. Homer Buckman, locksmith and odd-job man, dressed in worn overalls, iron filings and wood shavings sticking to his clothes. 'Killed Ol' Dan. Saw it happen. Lord, Lord!' His voice died away in wonder and horror.

'Maybe,' Mike Connor spoke, 'maybe one of us could get across the open space an' into the brush?'

'No Mike. No!' his wife interrupted him frantically. 'Don't think of it! For the love of God don't!'

There was an outburst of babbling.

'You wouldn' make it. Too far to go.'

'Maybe, though. By the livery stable. Where the brush is closest.'

'Naw. It'd be crazy. They got a man in the stable. He'd see ya.'

'They won't see him, because he isn't going!' Kate Connor, small and plump and plain, held on to her husband's arm. Childless, her man was all she had in the world.

'It's a chance, though,' a voice said from among the crowd. 'I mean, if a fella could get across the flat an' into the brush. The Conlon place ain't but ten mile from here. Get there in two-three hours, runnin'.'

'Then why don't you do it?' Kate Connor shouted in the direction of the voice. 'You think it's such a good idea, why don't we leave it to you?'

There was an awkward pause, then, 'It warn't my idea,' the voice mumbled.

Mike Connor, thirtyish, slightly built and gentle by nature, stood irresolutely, patting his wife's arm in ineffectual reassurance.

'Killed Old Dan,' murmured Homer Buckman again, unable to rid his mind of the idea. 'Heard his neck snap. In broad daylight. What kind of creature would do a thing like that? Lord, Lord, Lord! Rest Ol' Dan's soul an' have pity on us all.'

Lou Gans came along, slowly, bewilderedly,

stopping to look back down towards his store. His
assistant, Edie Stacey, followed him, like a dog
following sheep.

'They've taken over my store.' Lou spoke half to
the crowd, half to himself. 'Just took it over. Big
fella. Real mean one. They're gonna jus' help
themselves. Takin' ever'thing – clothes, boots – best
I got in stock, too. No money, no payment, nothin'.'
He looked in shocked incredulity at the uneasy
assembly before him and saw only his own shock
reflected back to him. 'Pullin' ever'thing out …
rippin' drawers open … lettin' stuff fall all over the
floor.' His eyes opened even wider in fear and
incredulity. 'Was gonna shoot me, when I grabbed
them Top-Deal shirts! Shoot me! Kill me! Woulda
done it too. An' all them shirts an' drawers an' vests
an' stuff, all over the floor. Walkin' over ever'thing.
In my own store – my own store! Mine!'

'They won't get the new Balbriggans, Lou –
Mister Gans.' His assistant corrected herself. About
thirty years old, Edie Stacey was lean, dark and
deep. She looked at her boss with a glance that was
at once admiring and calculating. 'I hid the new
bale behind the store-bin. Some 'Steader pants, too.
Hid 'em good. They won't see 'em. Woulda locked
the ladies' room too, if'n I'd had the key.'

'Well, what we gonna do, eh?' Ed Garside called
urgently. His face was swollen and disfigured from
the beating he had received from Holby. 'I mean
we jus' gonna stan' around here? They got my boy
in there, an' Tom Morrow's girl. An' that don't
mean they won't take other kids, or women, either.

Your Jack, maybe, Chris.' He nodded to a man beside him. 'Or your Cilly.' He nodded to a woman. 'So it ain't jus' me an' Mister Morrow. Now what we gonna *do*?' He moved jerkily in his distress and agitation, his hands gesticulating awkwardly. 'You all gotta help us! It ain't jus' us that's ...'

'We'll do it ourselves, Ed, if we have to – jus' you an' me,' said Tom Morrow. He too was moving unceasingly in his anxiety, a few paces one way, a few paces the other. 'We'll do *somethin'*. ... We jus' gotta think!'

There were troubled mutterings.

'But what *can* we do? They got all the weapons.'

'They're killers, real killers! Best do as they say.'

'But Jesus!' Jem Balmer spoke up the words forced out of him by tension. 'There's only six of them. There's 'bout twenty of us. Surely we could ...?' He looked around them, words running out on him.

'We could do what, Jem?'

'Yeah. Tell us what we could do.'

'What you got in mind, then?'

A number of men looked at him challengingly.

'Well, we could ... that is, maybe we could. ...' He stopped, words running out on him again. He snorted gently, gestured with his hands and shrugged his shoulders.

'There's nothing we *can* do but wait,' insisted Isaac Stone. 'We must wait for the Lord's deliverance. Hear me now, men – and women. The Lord will show us the way.'

'Poor ol' Dan!' murmured Homer Buckman.

'Terrible way to die. They killed him. ... Saw it happen. Poor ol' Dan.'

FOUR

He dragged himself out of his troubled half-sleep when the sun was low in the sky, rubbing his sore bones and casting fearful glances in the direction of the trail. Travelling at night was slow and difficult but he had no choice.

He took the reins and led the mule to where it could graze for a couple of hours before resuming his journey. Maybe he'd find something besides grass? Some wild turnips maybe? His empty belly clutched him like a cruel fist and his thin body trembled inside the shapeless prison clothes.

How long could he go on? How long could a man go, without regular food and sleep? Well, he'd been travelling – what? Week? Ten days? More? Less? He didn't know. There stretched behind him just a fevered dream of flight, of hunger, of snatched fragments of quarter-sleep when he hardly dared close his eyes for fear of the approaching hoofbeats, the triumphant voices, the fatal hand on his arm – because Krieg was after him and Krieg never gave up, never failed to bring his man back.

He winced as the mule, tearing at the grass, jerked at the reins, causing the fetter and chain on his wrist to gall the raw flesh. Maybe they were right! Maybe there was no escape, only death or going back. 'No!' He shouted the word aloud, in a sudden frightened yelp, causing the mule to start in alarm. No! Not that! Not that! He'd die first. He had the piece of broken saw-blade. His hand went to the rusty shard of metal stuck between the piece of rope that held up his pants around his skinny body. It was there: he wouldn't lose that. And he knew how to use it – crosswise, deep, under the ear, the way Koslowsky had shown him. An image flashed through his mind of Koslowsky lying crumpled on the latrine floor, curiously small and shrunken, blood congealing like glue all round him and that wide, ragged red rip in his neck. Strangely, there was no feeling of sorrow for Koslowsky: only relief, and a small weak kind of triumph, because Koslowsky had beaten them. Well, he could do that too, he knew he could and would. But not yet, because there was still a chance.

He watched the mule tearing at the grass. That was something they had on him now, definitely had on him: mule stealing. Yeah, but he'd *done* that. He'd definitely taken the mule. He hadn't liked the idea but he'd been desperate. Well, he'd try to return the animal when he'd got to. ...

Where the hell was he anyway? And was he any nearer the goddam place? He reckoned he knew the country for fifty miles around the place and he was damned if he recognized any landmarks.

And supposing – just supposing – he made it: how would they feel about him – Adam Ruthven, Luke Brenner, Isaac Stone – folks who had once been his friends, and their womenfolk – how would they regard him? Maybe they'd think he was guilty. Maybe they wouldn't want him there. They might even hold him, notify the law, get him sent back?

No! They couldn't! Not that; they couldn't do that because he wasn't going back; it wasn't a determination, or even a vow: it was a fact. He'd heard Isaac Stone say one time that there was only one certainty in life and that was death. Well, Isaac was wrong about that, at least as far as he, Dave Stacey, was concerned: there were two certainties for him: one was death and the other was that he wasn't ever going back to the State prison.

So why was he so scared? He couldn't properly answer that question but he reckoned anybody would be, not just him. Day after day on the run, estranged from ordinary people, close to starving, denied sleep, raw wounds and ... all *that* behind him. Chained to a wall. Like an animal. The beating up. In spite of his greatest efforts the memories rushed back, flooding his mind: the intimidation, the terror, the madness – and the ultimate, dehumanizing outrage. 'Aaaaaargh!' He gave a shuddering yelp and scrabbled uncontrollably on the ground for a few seconds, the noise forced out of him causing the mule to plunge in alarm. No, no, no, no, no! He punched violently at his own head in a crazy attempt to drive out the terrifying knowledge. He was away from all that.

And he wasn't going back. He'd never suffer that outrage again: he'd kill himself first.

Two hours later he was back on the trail, heading west in the faint starlight. After a couple of hours riding he hauled up the mule suddenly. That bend in the trail – and the big rock by the side? Was that familiar, or was he imagining things? Dared he hope? A few miles further on there was another bend, with a clump of pines, that also looked familiar. He drove the mule forward with insistent cuts from a hazel switch as the hope in his heart gave way to a new increased fear of Krieg, following behind in pursuit, dedicated to bringing him back.

That ... bastard ... Krieg! What kind of man was that, so totally lacking in compassion?

Around midnight, the clouds parted and the moon shone through and he saw it – that distinctive mound that folks called McKeag's Mountain. Now he knew where he was! About a hundred miles more; a hundred miles to go. He laid into the long-suffering mule again, forcing it forward, then he stopped. Better ease off a bit. Hundred miles was still quite a way. Didn't want the animal to founder. Just take it steady and he'd get there all right. And there'd be food, and rest and safety – and Edie.

Now that there was a real possibility of reaching his goal he let himself think about Edie. How would she react when she saw him? Would she – he was afraid to even think the question – would she want him back? Their marriage had never really worked. He had tried his best but it had gradually become clear that she was disappointed in him. Edie wanted things. Had something to do with her poor childhood maybe, but she wanted things – money, power, status – and a man who could grab life by the throat and wrest these things from it.

And what had she got? She'd got him! 'A nothin' man,' she had once called him in a fit of frustrated bad-temper. An ordinary fella, maybe even less than ordinary. He'd laboured ineffectually throughout his youth on his pa's hard-scrabble farm; had been turned down even for the goddam army during the Civil War, on account of his health. He'd gone west to see what he could make of it and had ended up as a hired man in a two-bit livery stable in a one-horse town. He'd thought he'd got his break when old Ike had died and left him the stable, but that hadn't impressed Edie either. 'A fallin'-down shack an' two skinny crowbaits!' she'd sniffed. 'Big deal!' No, there was no hiding from it: he wasn't man enough for Edie; wasn't hardly a man at all.

So how came people didn't see that, for Chrissakes? Him a rapist? Jesus! Anyone could see – anybody – that he wasn't the type, just wasn't the type. Edie knew he was a rabbit. Even old Ike had known. 'Dave would walk a mile to avoid trouble,' old Ike had often said. As for committing crime! Jesus! Didn't people have no sense? No goddam eyes?

His mind ran over the record again, the unbelievable turn that his life had taken. If he

hadn't ridden towards Blessington, following the
lead about a candy wagon for sale. ... He'd thought
he could make a little money on that deal. And if
that goddam horse hadn't spooked and thrown
him into a briar patch!

The unwelcome memories flooded back. The
men – fierce, furious, angry men – looking for the
man who had raped a fifteen-year-old-girl; his
unexplained presence in the area (it turned out
that he'd been given a bum steer: there was no
candy wagon for sale in the area). But there was
blood on his clothes and scratches on his face – and
he was a very frightened man. Well, he would be,
wouldn't he? With a crowd like that around him.
And so he'd bolted, and that had sealed it.

But Jesus Christ! For the girl herself to identify
him! Him! For Jesus's sake! He let the mule drag to
a stop, overwhelmed by shock, incomprehensibility
and despair. Jesus! He hadn't been within two
miles of that farm near Windy Hollow. But he
understood how it had been – a young girl, a child,
terrified, in a deep state of shock; a posse of fierce,
angry men, sure that they had caught the culprit;
his own disreputable appearance and his obvious
fear. They were red-hot to catch somebody and
they'd caught him and he fitted well enough so
they convinced themselves – because they *wanted* to
believe they'd got the man – and their certainty
communicated itself to the girl: they wanted her to
identify him and in her shocked state she had done
so. He'd been lucky not to be lynched.

But there'd been an amateur sheriff with them

and he'd avoided the rope. Then the trial, and State prison.

State prison. Jesus Christ! If it only *had* been! Unjust though it was, he could have served out his time in a proper prison. But he'd found out, like many other unfortunates, that it wasn't the State that ran prisons: it was the prisoners – or some of them, the worst kind, the most degenerate, the most depraved of human beings. Prison officials knew that the easiest way to control dangerous men was to let them have their way, as much as possible. Throw the weaker inmates to them, as you would throw a sick calf to a wolf pack to appease them and detract them from attacking the herd, or yourself. Then they get the message: *they* control the prison, inside, and life has its compensations for them. In this way the toughest prisoners control the less tough, so that, for the authorities, the number of prisoners to be controlled is fewer and those fewer are easier to manage; everyone finds his place and the resultant equilibrium leads to a tenable position.

Tenable – as long as you're not Dave Stacey or Leo Koslowky. Poor Leo. He couldn't live with it and now he was dead. But he, Dave Stacey, he'd got away. Incredible as it seemed he'd actually escaped. He looked around him to convince himself of this unlikely fact.

But for how long? Krieg was after him. Krieg, the relentless bounty hunter. And Krieg had never failed. That was his boast, his pride. Didn't care what it cost – the money didn't matter: it was his reputation that mattered. Nobody ever got away from Krieg. Nobody ever had. He dedicated his life to recapturing fugitives. It was his reason for being; the one activity which made life meaningful, and therefore possible, for him.

Stacey kicked and beat the mule again in a new surge of fear, pushing it ever forward towards his goal and whatever awaited him there.

The three men skulked in the main room of Mike Connor's cabin, taking advantage of the fact that Mike's wife was out somewhere, joined with other women in collective worrying. They came at the matter slowly, awkwardly, none of them really wanting to take the lead or knowing how, but feeling themselves pushed onwards by silent social pressures and not wanting to appear cowardly.

'If only we had a gun,' mumbled Mike. 'Jus' one gun even. Any kind. Would give us a chance.'

'Yeah. But we ain't.' Tom Morrow made the unnecessary response. 'We got to use other weapons – knife, club, maybe.'

'That means we got to get real close,' said Ed Garside.

'Yeah,' Morrow agreed again. 'But it's quieter. No one'll hear, hardly. We could take them one at a time.'

There was a noticeable silence while each of them envisaged that real and terrifying possibility.

'I figger a club of some kind,' said Tom Morrow, bringing the thing a step nearer to reality. 'Long club,' he comforted himself. 'You got some reach with that.'

'Knife might be better,' mumbled Mike Connor, thoughtfully. 'You can hide a knife – well, till the last minute. Then uuuuugh!' He grunted and made a short lunge. 'It's all over.' He hoped it would be.

'Knife, club, it don't matter. Long as we get them kids out,' said Ed Garside. 'I ain't leavin' my boy in there with the likes of them. Not much longer, I ain't. If they kill me, I ain't.' He had said it now and couldn't retract it.

'An' my girl too,' assented Tom Morrow warmly, encouraged by the uncertain resolution in Garside's voice. 'I owe it to that girl, an' my wife. Owe it to them.'

'When then?' Connor was carried along. 'When's the best time?'

'Tomorrow. Mornin'. Jus' after they've et. Or while they're still eatin',' claimed Morrow.

'Hell with tomorrow. Why not today? Tonight?' Garside was more confident now that it wasn't in the present but in the future. 'They been here three days now. My boy been in there three whole goddam days with them.'

'Naw,' insisted Connor. 'They're watchful at night, like as if they expected trouble, in the dark. Mornin's best. They're more relaxed in the mornin'. You know how it is yourself: you feel safer when the day comes – with the light, you know?'

'Awright, then. In the mornin',' Ed Garside agreed. 'But we ain't puttin' it off no longer, right?'

He felt as if he had passed sentence of death on himself, for the words chilled him as they came out of his mouth. He wished he hadn't uttered them but couldn't have stopped them from coming out.

Another uneasy meeting, this time amongst women, was taking place in Esme Grunfeld's home. Here, too, they couldn't come at the thing directly – wanted to, but couldn't – so there was nothing to do but come at it by the long, awkward route.

'I knew it would come to this. Jus' knew it. Knew it would.' Esme, with no daughters, shook her head in safe foreboding.

There was an awkward silence, then, 'Uh-huh. Guess so,' said Jane Mallen. 'Guess we all thought like that. Wonder, in a way, it's taken so long. They been here what? Three-four days?'

'Three.'

'But the leader fella – him with the sick brother – he said if we co-operated they wouldn' do nothing,' May Grant reasoned anxiously. 'An' we've done that. Give them food, clothes. Hain't made no trouble. No trouble at all.'

'It ain't him,' explained Jane Mallen again. 'It's the fella in the store, big dirty-blond fella. He's the one. Others ain't said nothin' – yit.'

'Mama, you won't send me!' Eighteen-year-old Greta Gregg broke in, in a fearful panic. 'Promise! Promise you won't, Mama?' Her round plump face was a shade paler than usual though it still reflected the confident assumption that her wishes would be granted, as they always were.

'Hush, hush!' muttered her mother, reaching out and patting her arm, the nearest she could get to reassuring her without openly declaring it and antagonizing the others.

'Well, ain't none of my girls goin'.' Lorna Miller came out strong, forced on by a mixture of fear and determination. 'They ain't. Not my Betty nor Jane. I'd go myself first,' she added, to take the edge off her comment and make it more acceptable to the others.

'He won't have that,' said Jane Mallen hopelessly. 'He'd throw you out. Nancy Bryson took his vittles up yesterday. He threw her out. Says it's got to be a young girl. Says if we don't send a young girl with his vittles he's a-comin' out to pick for hisself an' he's likely to pick two or three.'

'But we should tell his boss – the leader fella – he'd make him stay in there,' Maud Taylor argued anxiously.

'Mr Stone tried that, an' the boss fella said he'd see to it. But seems like the big fella in the store don't take orders good. Isaac said the boss fella can't really control him. An' he ain't too worried anyhow: jus' worried 'bout his brother who's sick.'

'Well my girls ain't goin'!' Lorna Miller repeated, making the situation crystal clear. 'I don't care what. They jus' ain't. Don't care what happens!'

'Well my Greta ain't goin' neither, if it comes to that!' Lean, gimlet-eyed Letty Gregg could stake her own claim strongly now. Her plump, spoiled daughter looked relieved, and being relieved could take some interest in the business now. Her eyes went to Annie Slocum, the nineteen-year-old orphan who drudged for her mother in the home and in their dairy. Annie, drab in shapeless homespun and gunny sack apron, but not unpretty, shrank back into her corner, picking her fingernails in anxiety, the sense of foreboding swelling frighteningly inside her.

'Maybe Annie could go?' Greta Gregg's plump pasty face took on an expression of sincere reasonableness.

'Oh, please, Mrs Gregg!' the servant girl begged hoarsely, her face grey and drawn. 'Don't ask me that. Please! Please! I'll do anything....'

'Well my Amy ain't goin' an' that's a fact!' May Grant rushed in with her claim.

'Well don't think any of my girls is goin'!' insisted Maud Taylor. 'Since everybody is stakin' their claim.'

Annie Slocum began to cry, feeling the tide turning against her. Mrs Miller, mother of eighteen-year-old Donna and seventeen-year-old Fay, turned towards her, sensing a useful compromise.

'Now, Annie,' she began, 'Mrs Gregg been real good to you. Took you in when you had nobody, remember – had no place to go. An' she gives you a good home. Looks after you.' She didn't say that the cost to the girl was her life, her freedom, her dignity. 'You oughta think of that. Folks can't jus' go takin', takin', takin' all the time. Got to do somethin' in return, time to time.'

'I know, ma'am, I know that – an' don't think I

don' appreciate it.' The words tumbled out of the frightened girl. 'But I couldn' do that. I couldn'. Go in there … with that man. … I couldn', honest, I couldn'. I'll quit the town first, go away from here. It ain't that I'm ungrateful, Mrs Gregg, but I jus' couldn'. …'

'Well my girls ain't goin'!' Lorna Miller was adamant now.

'An' neither are mine.' May Grant was equally certain. 'No way they ain't goin'!'

'Now Lorna, May! Please! Let's not fight. It's a hard time for all of us, 'thout that.' Esme Grunfeld tried to pour oil on the troubled waters.

There was a troubled silence. It lasted for a long time, then Mrs Miller spoke again. 'You know Mrs Gregg been good to you, girl.' She looked hard at Annie Slocum.

'Yes'm. I know that. But please! Please! I won't ask no more – from anybody. I'll quit. Go away from here. Find another place.'

'Why that's crazy, girl!' snapped her employer and protector. 'You know you can't do that. There ain't no way out of the town now.'

Annie Slocum looked in desperate appeal at the faces of the women surrounding her but found nothing there to reassure or comfort her.

FIVE

He left the mule outside the canyon. Better not take it close to the houses. Goddam critter might wake everybody up, and he didn't want a public reception. Not yet. Better go slow, wait till he knew how they felt about him. He'd try to contact Joe first. Joe Gregory. The blacksmith. He and Joe had been friends – well, kinda friends. And he'd need Joe's help to get rid of the manacle and chain. He could hardly imagine how it would feel not to have that agonizing handicap dragging on the end of his arm.

Would Joe help him? He could only hope so. It was true that they had been kinda friends – just kinda, because neither he nor Joe was the type to make friends easily. Joe was a bit like himself, he reckoned: a bit of a rabbit and therefore apprehensive of making approaches to people, even friendly approaches. It was strange how much he had learned about himself in the past couple of years. The result of his experience, he supposed. Well, if that was how experience and self-knowledge were gained they could keep it. But right now he had to approach Joe. Had no choice.

Although there were still about two hours to go before dawn there was a light in the livery-stable window. In his window. That stable is mine, he thought to himself, crouching down in the dark about two hundred yards away. It belongs to me. Old Ike Burgess left it to me. An' I got two horses in there – or I had, couple of years ago. And now somebody else is sittin' in there.

Maybe it's Edie, he thought, but he dismissed the idea instantly. Whatever you might say about Edie she wasn't the type to sit up all night in a stable.

He stole forward with great caution. There'd be dogs around – that goddamned great wolfhound of Jem Balmer's. And others too, smaller, but just as noisy. Maybe they'd know him, know his scent? Would dogs remember for two years? He'd prefer not to find out, right now, anyway.

It was strange to be approaching his own home like this, like a goddam thief in the night. Town hadn't changed a bit, far as he could see in the dark. Same buildings, in the same places. How many times had he dreamed of it, lying heart-broken in that hellish cell during those long, fear-shredded nights! The reality of his prison experience came back to him with chilling clarity, causing him to shiver uncontrollably, so that he had to stop and sink down on to the earth, temporarily unable to function. Christ! Was it that bad? And was *he* that bad? Would he be able to go through with it?

Yeah. He would. He felt again for the metal

shard stuck in his cord belt. There was always that – if it came to the worst. But he'd made it this far, and he was still free. Now if only Edie would fall in with it. If she would accept him, agree to come away with him. He could get his two horses ... and as much of their stuff as they could carry ... and they could ride west. There was lots of space out there, lots of places – places where hardly nobody had been – white folks, anyways. Even Krieg couldn't track him there, couldn't follow him forever, surely to Jesus? He dragged himself half-upright again and made his stealthy way to the stable window.

There was a man in there, sure enough, and at the very first sight of him his heart sank.

He knew him. Not the individual, not his name: it was the type he recognized: the man was a criminal, a violent criminal. Two years of hell permitted the watcher at the window to recognize the body language, the expression, the features, the whole aura that seemed to surround the slouching figure. He could have been Scalp Hoggart, or Hefti Barr, or Fenwick or Delders or any of those murderous diseased *wrong* men who had dominated the State prison, and at the very sight of him his heart faltered and he actually sank to the ground in an overwhelming silent despair.

He'd made his great effort, the greatest effort of his life, and he'd travelled two hundred agonizing miles – only to find what he'd thought he'd left behind confronting him again. What in the name of God was he to do now?

He did not know how long he lay on the damp earth but after a while found himself in the shed next to Joe Gregory's forge, sitting on a pile of cold iron, surrounded by stacked wood and sacks of charcoal and weighing the manacle-chain in his two hands. He must have made his way there subconsciously, the idea of Joe and the removal of the chain active in his mind. Must have been that, because there was no other idea in his mind. His mind was blank. He had absolutely no idea of what to do next.

What was such a man doing in Blake's Canyon? Because he didn't belong there. He knew in his bones that the man was a wrong one – and his instinct told him that such men do not operate singly: where there was one there would be others. What were they doing there? And how was their presence going to affect his plan?

Maybe they were waiting for him? Maybe they'd known he'd come here and they'd beaten him to it. Wouldn't have been hard. Was Krieg here too? Was he lost already? Damned? Was it time to use the shard of broken saw blade?

Naw. Not yet. That was the very last move. And the time for the last move was not yet. Wait. When you couldn't do nothin', couldn't make a move, then wait. He'd learned that. He'd wait – and see what happened.

Nothing happened for nearly three hours. Day came and Blake's Canyon seemed to be sleeping late – a very unusual thing to happen. Something was wrong. The place *felt* wrong. Nobody moving, an hour after daylight! Where was Joe Gregory? Joe was always an early starter. Usually up before dawn, tapping and hammering away in his forge at one of his crazy 'inventions'. Lou Gans, too. He was another one. He'd always be in his store, right from the very start of the day. And Reuben Watts, and Adam Ruthven, to say nothing of the womenfolk. Where was everybody?

Another hour dragged past and little happened. Smoke rose from one or two chimneys and the smell of cooking drifted on the air making his belly gripe with emptiness. A door creaked. He peered out of the doorway of the shed, and saw the livery-stable door open. The man inside, a big, fat man, shoved out into the day, dragged open his fly and pissed blatantly out into the street. In Blake's Canyon! In the middle of the morning! What in the hell was going on?

As Stacey quickly withdrew into the cover of the shed again he heard slow hoofbeats, a horse walking. A rider came down the street. Another stranger, a young man, hard-looking, wearing a Confederate kepi and a crazy kind of grin. 'Buff?' the rider called. 'Cammil?' He checked the horse and stepped down from the saddle, leaving the animal ground-haltered.

'Yeah?' The fat man from inside the stable shoved his way out to the doorway.

'Come to relieve ya. Give ya a break.'

The fat man nodded sullenly. 'Bout fuggin' time.' He shoved the younger man aside and nodded up the street. 'Hey! Look!'

Three men had come round one of the
buildings, about fifty yards away. One had a
pickaxe handle in his hands and one a billet of
wood. The other appeared to be empty handed but
he carried one arm rather stiffly by his side. The
man in the shed knew them: Ed Garside, Tom
Morrow and Mike Connor.

'Hey! Where the fug you think you're goin'?'
The fat man in the stable door shouted to them.
His partner laughed crazily, drew a pistol and
started to walk towards them.

The three men stopped. They clearly hadn't
expected anyone to see them. They looked at each
other quickly, almost frantically. Then Ed Garside
broke away from them and dropping his axe
handle ran back the way he had come. Tom
Morrow stood for a second longer then he also
took flight. Chuckling crazily the young man with
the kepi and the drawn pistol began to run after
them, lithely, eagerly.

The remaining townsman, Mike Connor, hesitated only a moment then seemed to decide on a
different tactic. He dropped a long kitchen knife
that he had been concealing and ran heavily in the
other direction, dodging between two buildings
and breaking into open space, heading for the
brush about a hundred and fifty yards away, as
though hoping to find sanctuary there.

The fat man in the stable door watched him go,
then he moved with surprising swiftness to the
horse standing nearby. With a bound he was in the
saddle and kicking the startled animal into a

sudden gallop. 'Heeeeeeeh – haaaaaah!' he cried, splitting the morning air with a fierce cowboy yell.

The running man looked round, saw him coming after him and continued to run, desperately trying to increase speed.

The galloping horse was quickly overtaking him. The fat rider felt and saw a long scabbard bouncing and swinging wildly from his saddle – the bayonet that Johnny Reb habitually carried there. With another joyous whoop he withdrew the blade and brandished it aloft as he rode down the fleeing man.

Mike Connor did not look round again but blundered frantically in a straight line for the brush, desperate to reach cover. But he heard and felt the drubbing hoofbeats rapidly gaining on him.

The watcher in the shed rushed to the back of that building and, peering through a chink between two boards, saw it all happen.

The fat man on the galloping horse rode up carefully alongside the running man. Checking his horse, he kneed it right alongside the fugitive and brought the heavy bayonet down on the man's head. The watcher in the shed heard the 'Klunk' as the blade struck the unprotected skull.

Mike Connor staggered then swerved involuntarily and continued his run in another direction, but staggering badly as though disoriented. A jerk on the reins, a shift of the body in the saddle, a stab with the spurs and the rider was alongside him again. A vicious hack with the bayonet as he swept past. Connor's hands went upwards to his head in a vague, protective gesture as he staggered even more wildly. Another cut with the blade as the arm returned from the swing, another 'Klunk'. Connor swerved again and stumbled, all sense of direction or purpose obviously having left him. He reeled about like a badly drunken man, staggering, almost falling, his groping hands reaching vaguely upwards for his head and not succeeding in finding it. The mounted man had stopped his horse now and just kept it prancing, sidling around, watching to see how the wounded man would move now.

Connor stumbled a few shaky steps. A stab with the spurs, a lunge of the horse and another 'Klunk'. Now the rider waited for the next move.

There was none. Mike Connor simply stood still for a couple of seconds, looking bewildered, blood pouring down his face and arms, then he crumpled up and sank slowly to the ground. The man on the horse watched him for a moment as if calculating whether he might get up again, then hauled his horse round and rode at a walk back into the huddle of buildings. As he rode past the shed he thrust the heavy bayonet back into its scabbard. His hands were red and sticky with blood. A small crowd, drawn by the noise, was standing watching, silent and rooted to the spot.

The man in the shed watched, stupefied. He heard voices calling from up the street somewhere. 'Cammil? Johnny? What the fug is it? What's goin' on?'

'It's OK, Maxie,' the fat man called. 'Jus' a smart bastard tryin' to make a break for it. He's given it up – for now, anyways.'

The younger man, the one with the kepi, came walking back casually, holstering his pistol. 'They got away,' he grinned. 'But jus' back inside the houses. They didn' go noplace.'

'Hey you!' the fat man shouted towards the small knot of people who had watched the brutal action, 'Where the fug you think you're goin'?' A woman was walking out into the open area surrounding the buildings, walking towards the man who had been cut down. It was Kate Connor.

'I'm goin' to my man.' She paused to reply then continued on her way.

'You stay where you are, ya hear me? Leave that fuggin' fella where he is.'

Kate Connor walked on as though he had not spoken. When she reached the fallen man she sank down on to the earth beside him and put her arms around him. After a few minutes she turned and looked towards the small crowd. 'Somebody give me a han',' she called. 'Help me get my man back to his own place.'

'You stay where you fuggin' are!' shouted the fat man.

Two women started forward and then stopped, hesitating.

'Please!' called Mrs Connor. 'Please! I can't do it myself.'

The two watching women hesitated a further moment, then one walked forward, steadily, to help her. The other followed too, after a few seconds more. Between them they began to half-carry, half-drag Mike Connor back towards the buildings.

The man called Cammil swore under his breath, hefting his pistol in his hand, then he holstered the gun and turned to walk up the street. 'Serve the bastard right,' he muttered.

The unseen man in the shed found himself sitting on the pile of cold iron again. Jesus Christ! Was he going mad? Was he? Was that the explanation? It seemed the only one that would fit. Or maybe he had died and was now in hell?

He sat and wondered, silently, stunned by events. What in God's name was happening in the world? Again the possibility that he might be mad presented itself to him.

But he didn't think so. There were some things he recognized. Those people – Isaac Stone, and Mike Connor, and Ed Garside and the others. They were real. He knew them. They looked like that. And this was his town, his home, Blake's Canyon. And he'd been in prison for over two years. He looked at the moist flesh of his right wrist, raw-red and black with dirt. That was real: he felt the pain of it. No. He wasn't mad. The things around him were real, they were happening. But what ...? How ...? He couldn't even begin to think. He could only wait for some kind of understanding to come to him.

He waited a long time. The small crowd of people drifted away, the street became silent once again – completely silent, unnaturally so – and the hunger-gripe started to twist his guts again, more cruelly than ever. Jesus! He'd have to do something. Kreig was behind him. But his way forward was blocked.

The sound of hoofbeats approached. He peered through a chink in the boards. Joe Gregory. Leading a couple of horses. Coming towards the forge. Joe. The man he wanted to see. Had to speak to. Would he get the chance?

Joe Gregory led the horses up to the back door of the smithy and dropped the reins, ground-haltering them. He bent down slowly, as if in some kind of daze, and picked up one of the animal's feet and studied it.

'Psssssst! Joe!' The watcher called. And before Joe could respond: 'Joe! Hey! Joe! Over here! In the shed!'

Gregory dropped the hoof and glanced around, nervous, frightened. He rose and began to move towards the forge, as though to escape from any kind of dangerous involvement.

'Joe! It's awright! It's me! Dave Stacey!' In his fear of losing his opportunity the man in the shed stepped out into view. 'Joe! It's only me!' He touched himself with both hands as though to emphasize his reality to the other man.

Gregory stopped and his mouth actually dropped open in fright and amazement. He stood still, gawping.

Stacey retreated a step back into the cover of the shed. 'Joe, c'mere! I need you, Joe. I gotta talk to you. Please! Naw! Don' turn away, Joe. Please. I need you.'

Gregory paused in his half turn, cast a frightened glance towards the forge then seemed to take a decision in his mind. He turned back and plodded the few steps to the shed.

They were both inside the shed now, in the dull gloom.

'Dave? Dave Stacey? Is it you, honest? What you doin' ...?' Gregory stared uncomprehending at the man before him, bewildered by the flapping prison clothes, the manacle and chain, the wildly long hair, the emaciated appearance. 'They aint let you out?'

'Naw. Escaped. But it's okay, Joe. I'm goin' away. Won't make no trouble for ya.' He spoke in urgent whispers. 'But I need your help, Joe. Say you'll help me. I'm goin' away, Joe. Far away. Won't nobody know I've been here. But I need your help. You'll help me, Joe?'

Gregory was still shaking his head in slow wonder. 'We're the ones as needs help,' he said. 'Things is ... all changed here ... Dave. ...' He said his name as though it was a strange, new word.

'Joe, I don't understand. But I got to get this manacle off ... an' chain. An' I want to see Edie. Get my horses an' stuff. But those men ...?'

'Gang of some kind,' murmured Gregory, still staring at him uncomprehendingly. 'Came here few days ago. Took over the place. Killed Ol' Dan Pender.' Gregory was plainly in a state of shock. 'They got a sick man. In Ben Partlin's place. How'd you get out?' He was slow and confused.

'That don't matter. I got out. An' I only want to get away. Goin' west. Far west.'

'It's real dangerous. They got a fella in there.' He nodded towards the forge. 'An' another fella in the store. An' in the stable – your ol' place. Rest is in Ben Partlin's house. With the sick man. They're killers. Real killers. You got no idea. You know they cut Mike Connor down this mornin'? Hacked him to the groun'. Don't seem likely he'll live. You ain't got no idea. …'

'Oh, yeah, I have, Joe. Believe me, I have. But I got to get this chain off. There's a fella behind me, Joe, a bounty hunter. I gotta get my horses an' stuff and get on, Joe. Will you do it for me, Joe? Please, Joe? For ol' times' sake?'

Gregory was looking at the manacle on his wrist. 'There's a fella in there.' He nodded again towards the forge. 'One of 'em. Big fella. Mean. They're all big. An' mean.'

'I got to get in there, Joe.' In his anxiety Stacey moved out of the shed, a few steps in the direction of the forge. Gregory moved with him, half consciously, then he turned and seizing Stacey by the arm dragged him back towards the shed.

'What you doin'?' he muttered anxiously. 'Didn' you hear me? They got a man in there. Why these fellas would kill you – I mean *kill* you – jus' as soon as look at you.'

'I know. You tol' me. But I got to get this chain off. I got to, Joe. You'll help me, huh? I got to get away, Joe. Goin' west. Long way off. Jus' as soon as I see Edie – an' get our stuff. …'

'You can't go in there.' Gregory's voice was low and hoarse. There was also a note of growing anger in it. 'You can't, I tell you. 'Tain't jus' you. They got a coupla kids ... they're holdin' hostage. You do anythin' to make 'em angry an' they're liable to kill those kids. That what you want?'

Stacey pulled up, shocked. 'They got kids? Hostages?'

'Yeah. You do anythin' an' them kids could get killed.'

'Jesus.' Stacey shook his head in incredulity. 'Jesus. What am I gonna do? I got to get this thing off. Got to see Edie. Get our stuff, an' horses. Get out of here. 'Fore Krieg catches up on me.'

'You can't do it here. Ain't no way you can.' Gregory looked almost relieved: this way he would be off the hook.

Stacey paused for a few seconds then looked straight at him. 'I got to. Got to, that's all. Can't go no further, 'thout gettin' this manacle off ... an' 'thout gettin' horses an' stuff.'

'You can hide here.' Gregory was very frightened. 'Like the rest of us. Till they're gone. I'll try to git you some vittles. Might not be long. ...'

'Naw. I can't. Krieg's behind me. Bounty hunter. He'll come here ... bound to.' Stacey shook his head in dread. 'Naw. I got to get this iron off. An' you got to help me Joe.' He took a couple of steps towards the door of the shed.

Gregory was after him in a flash. 'You can't, I tell ya! They got men all over the place – forge, stable, store, ever'place! You want to get them kids killed?'

Stacey turned on him. 'I got to get away, Joe. Them kids ... they ain't dead, yet ... they still got a chance. ... But me? I ain't got no chance, no chance at all. I *am* dead. Unless I get my stuff an' move on.' He moved out of the doorway and towards the smithy door. 'I got to get away, 'cause I ain't goin' back. ...'

'What about them kids? What about them, huh?' Gregory was following him in his anxiety, pulling at his arm. They were both making too much noise. 'You more important than them kids?' They were close to the forge door now, but in their anxiety they did not hear the approaching footsteps.

Stacey half turned again, his voice rising in his anxiety. 'Joe, I told ya. "I ain't goin' back, Joe. I ain't ever goin'. ..."'

The forge door swung open. The man, Mako, stood there, face twisted in annoyance. 'Say what the fug's goin' on?' he snarled. 'Who the fug's this? What the fug d'ya think ...'

There was a loud 'Klunk' as the square plate on the end of Stacey's manacle-chain struck him fiercely on the forehead. He staggered a few steps and stood dazed for two seconds, blood starting to trickle freely from his head. Stacey leapt towards him. He lifted the end-plate of his manacle-chain in both hands and brought it down frantically on Mako's head. Once, twice, three times. Gregory stood petrified, hearing the dull thuds. Mako sagged, collapsed. Stacey dealt him another murderous blow to the head. Mako's face was a mask of blood. He lay silent and unmoving.

'Help me get him inside.' Stacey's face was working uncontrollably, his voice breaking. He looked as if he too would collapse at any minute. He grabbed Mako under the armpits and began to drag the heavy limp body towards the open door of the forge. He wasn't strong enough. 'Help me, for Christ's sake, Joe,' he begged.

Gregory found himself carrying Mako's feet. He too was trembling violently and the idea came to him that his life was fast approaching a violent conclusion.

SIX

'Did anybody see us?' Stacey called nervously from his position on the floor of the forge beside the sprawled form of Mako.

'Don't think so.' Joe Gregory peered anxiously from the corner of the glassless window. 'Lord above us! We were lucky. In broad daylight, too. But the place is quiet; folks not movin' aroun' much.' He turned away from the window, wringing his work-calloused hands. 'Lord God of Hosts!' he prayed. 'What are we gonna do now? See what you've done!' He stared at Stacey in wonder. 'Jus' see what you've done.'

'I couldn' help it. Honest. I jus' ... hit out.' Stacey's nervous condition was as bad as Gregory's. He panted for breath and trembled visibly. 'He came on us so quick-like. I hadda do somethin'. Couldn' jus' ... jus'. ...' He was unable to complete the sentence. He took a deep, shuddering breath. 'I was scared. Scared to death. I hadda do somethin'.'

'But what we gonna *do*?' Gregory's round, child-like face was blank with wonder. 'What are *they* gonna do – when they find out? Oh God! You done it now, Dave. You really done it. Lord God of ...'

'Oh quit it Joe, willya?' Stacey yelped. 'That ain't gonna help, jus' ... jus' sayin' that.'

Gregory jumped with fright at the sound, his babble drying up. They stood over the prone form, in the dusty gloom of the forge. A bar of sunlight sliced through a gap in the log wall, dust motes dancing in the beam.

'They ain't nobody seen us,' Stacey began again. 'An' I know what I have to do. Same as before. I got to get this chain off my arm. An' get my horses an' stuff. An' get my wife. An' get far away from here.'

'Yeah – but what about us?' demanded Gregory. 'Us that's left? What you're gonna do could get us killed.'

'Maybe ... maybe not.' Stacey was trying to collect his wits. 'But you understan' my position, Joe. I *got* to get these things, or else I'm dead. There's a *chance* that you can all survive but for me there ain't no chance; if I don't get that stuff, I'm dead. 'Sides,' he rushed to forestall Gregory's next remark, 'maybe we can beat these fellas, this gang.'

'Yeah? An' how? How we gonna do that?' Gregory was angry as well as scared. 'They got all the guns. They got kids as hostages. An' they're killers. You an' me, we're jus' ordinary folks. Ain't the fightin' type at all.'

'Hold it, Joe! Hold it a minute!' Stacey laid a hand on the other man's arm. 'Let's try to keep calm, huh? We ain't gettin' noplace like this. Now look, how many men are in this gang?'

Gregory thought for a moment. 'Six. Well, five – 'cause one is sick, sick bad.'

'Five.' Stacey reflected. 'Naw. Four.' He glanced down at the still form on the floor. 'Jus' four now. An' there's over a dozen men here in Blake's Canyon.'

'Yeah. But what kinda men? An' what about guns? What you say don't change all that.'

'Well, maybe,' said Stacey. 'But maybe we can do somethin'. Now, you gonna help me get this iron off?'

Gregory shrugged, glad to turn to something more tangible. 'Well, guess I can do that. Won't make no difference whether that's on or off.'

'The noise won't bring nobody roun'?'

'Don't think so. I been told to shoe their horses. They'll be expectin' some noise. But what about him?' Gregory nodded towards the limp form on the floor. 'He alive? Or is he ...?' He could not bring himself to say the word.

Stacey bent down and examined the body. 'I don't know. Can't be sure. He's still warm, but can't really tell if he's breathin'. But,' he glanced round, 'got any rope? I'll tie him up – 'case he comes round at an awkward time.' He took a length of dusty rope that Gregory handed him and bound Mako hand and foot. Mako began to make soft, snoring noises; blood ran from his nose and mouth. Stacey turned away hurriedly. 'Right, let's get this accursed thing off,' he urged.

Ten minutes later he was free of it. He stood beside Gregory at the anvil and rubbed the raw flesh of his wrist.

'Lord God of Hosts!' breathed Gregory in wonder. 'They did that to you?' He looked at the spike that had fixed the base plate to the wall. 'However did you get that out?'

'I dug it out. With two-three horseshoe nails. Bit at a time. Patched it up with mud to hide the damage during the days – mud made from earth and piss. Took me three months.'

Gregory was regarding him with wonder and horror. 'Dave?' He hesitated. 'Can I ask you somethin'? You don' mind? I mean you won't. ...'

'Go on, ask me.'

'Well ... what you done. ... What they said you done. ... That girl.'

'You want to know did I do it?'

Gregory said nothing, just kept looking at him.

'Jesus, Joe! You think I might have done it; don't you? You think it's possible. An' you *know* me! You know me – an' you think it's possible that I ...'

'Now look! I didn' say,' Gregory rushed in. 'Didn' say nothin'. An' anyway, who can say what any man will do? Sure I know you, but does any man really know any other man – I mean enough to know what he'll do an' what he won't do?' Gregory turned away, shaking his head.

'Well, I didn't do it. I goddam well didn't. Wasn't nowheres near that place. But if *you* think I mighta done it how in hell could I hope to convince those men – those strangers – that I didn't?'

'Okay, okay! You didn'. I believe you,' nodded Gregory. 'So what do we do now?'

Stacey rubbed the back of his hand over his eyes. 'You got anythin' to eat? Any goddam thing at all?'

'Naw. Not here. Sorry. But I guess I could get you somethin'. They expect me to move aroun' a little, in my work. I'll try.'

'Then do that, Joe, please. I'm gonna faint with hunger, else. An' Joe? Will you see Edie for me? Tell her I'm here, want to see her – but be careful, Joe: don't tell too many people. You don' know how they'll feel about me, an' about ... all this.'

'Don't worry 'bout that,' breathed Gregory, moving towards the door. 'I'll be careful all right. Lord God, I'll be careful.'

'So what was all the fuggin' noise about?' Max Slievan poured two glasses and stuck the cork back in the bottle.

'Aw, nothin'. Nothin' much.' Buff Cammil rested his great backside on the kitchen table and reached for the whisky. The eyes of Sarah Partlin went to the bottle – their whisky, which they never touched themselves but kept for medicinal purposes. She hoped they wouldn't get drunk. God knew what they'd be like drunk: they were dreadful creatures sober.

'There was a crowd down there. Some shoutin'.'

'Yeah.' The fat man grinned. 'Fella tried to run for it.'

'You stopped him?'

The fat man winked and cocked his head to one side in a gesture of affirmation. 'I stopped him.' He took another slug of his whisky.

'Stupid bastard,' grunted Slievan. 'Ya can't tell 'em nothin'. Too goddam stupid to learn. You kill him?'

'Naw.' The fat man shook his head. 'His ol' lady is tryin' to put him together again, but I reckon there might be bits of him still missin'.' He banged his whisky glass on the table and moved over to the doorway that connected the eating room to the sleeping room. 'How's ol' Abe doin'?'

Ben Partlin's bald head bobbed up from the bedside where he had been squatting beside the sick man. His grey face grew even more fearful when he beheld the fat man in the doorway. His lips moved but the sound that came out was inaudible.

'Yeah, jus' how *is* ol' Abe doin'?' Slievan followed Cammil to the doorway, brushed past him and paused half-way to the bedside.

'He's ... he's ... I think he's. ...' Ben Partlin moved about nervously, a very frightened man, quite unable to be still. 'He's sleepin', right now.' His voice quavered. 'I think I'll get. ...' He moved away from the bed, away from the two big men, trying to escape temporarily from the threat of their presence.

Slievan's big paw clamped on his arm and stopped him dead in his tracks. A couple of steps forward and he had hauled him back to the bedside. 'I said how *is* ol' Abe doin'?' The face looking down on the little man was full of the threat of violence and pain.

'Mister, I keep tellin' you, I ain't no doctor – wish

I was, but I ain't. My wife either. We ain't. We're jus' ordinary folks.'

'Shuddup! Ya hear?' Slievan shook him like a rat and the little man jerked till his teeth rattled. 'You're the medical man aroun' here. Ever'body says so. You treat people that's sick.'

'Only do what I can.' The little man was breathless and desperate. 'What anybody else could do. I can't cure folks. Can't save them from dyin'.'

'Well you'll fuggin' save Abe from dyin'!' Slievan's voice was a roar. 'You'll save my brother from fuggin' dyin'!' He shook the little man into a state of speechlessness. 'Hear me? You'll save Abe from dyin'.' The little man continued to be shaken until he looked like a silly doll. 'Because if you don't, mister. ...' The shaking stopped. Slievan grabbed Ben Partlin by the shirt collar with such force that the thick material tore with a loud ripping sound. He hauled the terrified face level with his own. ''Cause if you don't, by Christ you'll be sorry. You'll be goddam fuggin' sorry. An' not jus' you either. That goddam wife of yours. Her too, ya hear? You got no idea what we'll do to her.' He flung the little man away from him. 'Now get that fuggin' woman in here.'

She was already there. In the doorway, watching. Like her husband, she too was afraid, terrified. But behind the fear there was something else – just a spark, but present – a spark of anger, of rage, of concern for the wretched little man that was her husband.

'We're doin' all we can, mister. Doin' what we'd

do for one of own.' She came into the room. 'Can't
do no more'n that.'

'What the fug's wrong with him?' roared Slievan.
There was a note of something like fear in his voice,
mixed in with the anger.

'We don' know.' It was the woman who spoke
again. She was standing beside her man, her little,
balding, shaken, frightened man. She was holding
his arm, supporting him as much as she could.
'Could be anythin'. Pneumonia, maybe. Anythin'.'

'Well, you take care of him, ya hear?' Slievan's
voice was a bluster now, the voice of a man who
knows that the situation is out of his hands. He
looked down at the sick man, a silent, unmoving
figure in the bed, and then turned and moved back
to the other room, taking Cammil with him. 'You
get some chow, Buff,' he muttered, 'then go back to
the stable. Take over from Johnny. What about
Mako, an' Holby? They okay?'

'Yeah. Guess so.'

'They gettin' fed, an' all like that?'

'Yeah. They're gettin' fed,' the fat man grunted
as he clumped down the steps and out into the dirt
street. 'Ain't had no "all like that" yit. That's still to
come. Pretty soon, I reckon.' He grinned back
lewdly and waddled away.

The two men rode into the huddle of buildings just
before noon, the big steeldust and the chestnut
trudging stolidly side by side, the riders dusty and
travel-stained.

'You see if they got a drinkin' place,' mumbled

Krieg in his grudging monotone. 'Ask aroun' there. I'll enquire elsewhere. Meet you there.' He peeled his horse off to one side.

The town did have a saloon, a better one than a thirsty rider might have expected. Holborn looped the chestnut loosely to the rail and gratefully went in. It was cool inside, cool and damp-feeling, with the fine smells of beer and whisky heavy in the air. A few idlers sat around but little drinking was being done.

Holborn returned their nods of greeting as he moved to the bar. 'You got beer? Cool and wet?'

The bartender reached for a glass. There was a hoarse gurgling from a pump. 'It don't win no prizes.' The bartender looked at the beer as he pushed it across the bar. 'But I guess it'll wash your insides out.'

'This the place they call Huddledown?' Holborn looked at the other occupants over the rim of his glass before drinking.

'Yeah, this is it.' A friendly, anonymous voice. 'Ain't disappointed are ya?'

'Hell no.' Holborn lowered his glass and sighed with pleasure. 'Any place is welcome when you're on the trail.' They were studying his clothes, he knew, studying him, trying to figure out his angle.

'Come far?' asked an old man at a table back from the bar, an empty glass in front of him.

'Yeah. Long way.' Holborn was open, straight. 'Two hundred miles nearly. An' we got a way to go yet. Tryin' to catch up on some friends of ours, me an' my partner. We figger they're jus' a few days ahead of us. Anybody come through here past coupla days? Any strangers, I mean?' He motioned for the bartender to refill his glass.

'Naw. Nobody came through here,' ventured another man. 'Wrong time of the year for pilgrims.'

'Chummy Hope come by,' ventured another man. 'Whisky drummer. You know Chummy? Guess ever'body knows Chummy.'

Krieg entered and made his way to the bar in his lazy, heel-dragging manner. Holborn was going to order for him but remembered in time: Kreig always drank his own liquor.

'Naw it ain't the whisky drummer,' Holborn said, to keep the conversation going. 'I don't know Chummy but ...'

'We're huntin' an escaped con,' said Krieg, turning his bleak gaze on to the watching men. He pointed wordlessly to the beer pump and the bartender reached for a glass. 'Broke out of State prison, few weeks back, an' he ain't been through here.' He turned his back on the watching men and began to drink his beer.

Holborn felt uncomfortable. The local men had relapsed into silence. The gentle pleasure he had been experiencing in the casual conversation had disappeared completely. He would have liked to restart the conversation but felt that the locals weren't quite as friendly as before. And he certainly didn't want to chat with Krieg. He said nothing and just took another pull at his beer.

Later that afternoon, as they rode on their dusty

way, he reflected that riding with Krieg wasn't really agreeable: the comradeship, the easy conversation which would have compensated for the nuisance of the flies, the aching saddle-ass and the eternal jostle of horseflesh under them just wasn't there with Krieg. So Holborn gradually relapsed into silence. Krieg himself commented on the fact as they made camp that evening.

'You ain't sayin' much. Losin' your appetite for the work?'

Holborn paused in heaving his saddle from the warm back of the chestnut. 'I don' know that I ever *had* a great appetite for it. Jus' decided to give it a try, like I told you.'

Krieg's words came out in his dreary monotone. 'I can see you goin' back to bein' a deputy sheriff. Why did you quit that job anyway?'

Holborn unfastened the throat latch and pulled the bridle over the chestnut's ears. 'I didn't quit. I already told you. I got dropped.'

'Yeah? How come?'

Holborn clumped over and dumped his rig beside the small fire. 'They didn't like me – the people of Antler's Bend. Well, the people who mattered, people who gave out the appointments.'

'Thought you said you was a good lawman?'

'I was. Still say so.' He squatted by the fire and moved the blackened coffee pot closer to the blaze. 'Yeah. I was,' he continued thoughtfully. 'I believed in law. Still do. Figger there's things people should be allowed to do an' things they shouldn't be allowed to do. Things they oughta be punished for doin'.'

'You ain't tellin' me they fired you for that?'

'I keep tellin' ya. They didn't fire me. Jus' didn't renew my appointment. Got somebody else.' Holborn measured coffee into the now boiling water, sniffing pleasurably at the comforting aroma. 'Fact is, the people in power in Antler's Bend wanted two kinds of law. One kind for ordinary folks an' another kind, a different kind for themselves.' He dusted his hands and straightened up. 'They was all for being severe with ordinary offenders but when *they* did somethin' wrong – or their sons or daughters did – they wanted me to overlook it, give it a polite name, go easy on it.'

'You didn' think you oughta do that?' Krieg was standing by his horse, leaning on the saddle, making no attempt to remove his rig but just watching Holborn.

'Naw. Law's the law. Or it oughta be. Hard enough to decide what's justice, without havin' to consider who oughta get it.'

Krieg unfastened his cinches and heaved off his saddle. 'You think too much,' he grunted. 'That's your trouble.'

'Yeah. I been told that before,' replied Holborn philosophically, 'but I figger a man oughta think. Like I been thinkin' of this fella we're chasin'.'

'Ain't no need to think 'bout that.' Krieg was unusually emphatic. 'He's a con. He's escaped. We go after him and bring him back.'

Holborn had spread his blanket near the fire. He sat up now and began to fumble in the small gunny sack. He brought out the cold roast sowbelly and biscuits that they had bought in Huddledown that afternoon. He laid Krieg's portion on the spread out gunny sack and raised his own to his mouth. His white teeth tore off a piece of the greasy, heavily-salted pork and he chewed appreciatively for a moment. 'Yeah,' he said. 'That's one way of lookin' at it. But like I said, I been thinkin'. He always maintained he was innocent.'

Krieg gave a snort of disgust.

'Yeah, I know, they all do,' Holborn forestalled him. 'But this fella – Stacey, is it? Yeah – well, he don't seem like a criminal to me. From what I hear he had a real bad time in prison. Now you an' me,' he looked up at Krieg, 'we know how that can happen – an' jus' *what* can happen. An' we know the kinda men it happens to: it don't happen to your hard cases. Another thing: when this fella escapes, he don't go wild, shootin' people, holdin' up towns. He jus' tries to get back home. Like a kid.'

'He stole a mule.'

'Jesus, yeah!' Holborn sighed. 'He stole a mule. An' wouldn' you steal a mule if you was tryin' to get away from all that?' Holborn turned and faced Krieg, challenging him with his eyes.

Again Krieg gave his familiar snort of contempt. 'Like I said,' he grunted, 'you think too much.'

'Well, maybe. ...' Holborn tore off another hunk of sowbelly and recommenced chewing. Inside himself he added: An' you, Mister Krieg, you don't think enough. Don't hardly think at all.

SEVEN

When Gregory had gone Dave Stacey wandered uneasily around the forge. He leaned over the form of the man, Mako, on the ground. He was still unconscious and blood still flowed from his nose. Should a man be unconscious for so long? Or was he dying? Stacey didn't know. But he had done that! Him. Dave Stacey. He recoiled in horror at the thought and began moving aimlessly around the forge, unwilling to face what he had done. Besides, the central problem remained: he had to get his stuff and get away.

An idea struck him and, recoiling at the idea, he nevertheless went back to the prone form on the floor and removed the shell-belt and holstered pistol. He strapped it around his waist. He didn't know whether he felt better or worse. He had hardly ever worn a gun before.

He'd have liked a bandage for his wrist but there was nothing like that here: only piles of iron, horseshoes, wood and charcoal, bits of farm machinery, a few tools.

He rummaged absently on a bench – pincers,

rasp, files, a piece of an old buggy spring, strung with a wire and fitted with the stock of an old rifle – another of Joe's weird inventions probably – a few bolts, some scrap iron, lampblack for horses' hoofs, a can of tar. Nothing there he could use.

The door opened. Stacey whirled round, the curious spring-and-wire contraption still in his hands. Gregory stood in the doorway. 'Whatcha doin' with that?' Gregory's eyes were wide. 'That crossbow?'

'Huh? What?' Stacey was slow to understand. 'Oh, this?' He laid the curious implement down on the bench. 'Nothin'. Jus' picked it up.' He turned anxiously to Gregory for news. 'You got food, Joe? Did you see Edie? What did she say, Joe? Did you tell her?'

Gregory was emptying his pockets. 'Got a piece of rag for that wrist.' He laid a clean piece of cloth on the bench. 'An' a little food.' He brought out several biscuits, broken and crushed, and a big lump of fatty bacon.

Stacey fell on the food like an animal.

'Didn't see Edie. Couldn't find her.' Gregory was uncomfortable, but Stacey, cramming his mouth and chewing, did not notice.

'Fact is, Dave.' Gregory had picked up the curious spring-and-wire contraption and was awkwardly weighing it in his hands. 'Since you been away, Edie's been kinda ... well, you been away two years. Nobody thought ... none of us ... that you'd come back. An' Edie, well.' Gregory rested the weird contraption on his knee and looked directly at Stacey wolfing bread and meat. 'Well, Edie's kinda ... taken up ... with Lou Gans.'

Stacey's hunger was too great to permit him to stop eating altogether but his eyes met Gregory's. 'What do you mean? Taken up?' he mumbled through a mouthful of food. He swallowed and crammed his mouth again, his eyes frightened, worried.

'Well, like, I mean, she works for him – in the store. An' cooks for him sometimes too. An' well, like I say, she works for him. An' they go aroun' together, some.' Gregory's discomfort was obvious.

'She livin' with him?' Stacey stopped chewing. The words came out mangled and distorted, through a mass of half-chewed food.

'Naw. Naw.' Gregory replied hurriedly. 'Not really. It's jus' that, well, like I say, Dave, you was away a long time. Folks didn' think you'd ever come back. It ain't reasonable to expect. ...' He dried up into silence.

Stacey chewed and swallowed, lowering his hands to waist level. 'It figgers,' he said, and his tone was one of near despair. 'I mighta known. I shoulda thought of that. She wasn't to know I'd come back. 'Sides, I never was good enough for her.' He stared blankly ahead of him. 'Lou Gans, eh? Little fat, ugly Lou. But he's got a store, an' money, an' a future – an' lots of get-up-an'-go. Yeah, it figgers.' He attacked the bread and meat again, but less voraciously than before.

'But I'll see her all right,' Gregory assured him. 'I'll try again later.' He paused. Stacey was wolfing food again. 'What you gonna do now, Dave?'

Stacey laid the food down. Mouth still full, he began to wind the bandage that Gregory had brought round his mangled wrist. 'I don' know, rightly.' The words came out chewed, with little bits of expectorated food. 'I only know what I *ain't* gonna do: I ain't gonna let nobody take me back. Not ever.' He offered the end of the bandage to Gregory and motioned that he should tie it. Gregory obliged.

'I got to get into that store,' Stacey went on. 'Naw – nothin' to do with Edie or Lou. Got to get proper clothes, boots, supplies. Then I got to get my two horses … an' see Edie myself. Got to find out. An' then I got to get away from here.'

Gregory was shaking his head slowly. 'They got a man in there,' he said. 'Big fella. Real mean one. Armed, too. You can't go in there.'

'I got a gun now too.' Stacey indicated the holstered pistol that he had taken from Mako.

'Yeah. So I see. But you fire that gun an' you'll bring the rest of 'em runnin'. You forgot what I told ya? 'Bout the kids, the hostages? You daren't use that gun.'

Stacey shook his head in dismay. 'Jesus! Didn't think of that.' He reached for the food again and took another great bite. His eye fell on the spring-and-wire contraption in Gregory's hands. 'What's that thing? What didja call that?'

'This?' Gregory looked at it. 'It's a crossbow. I made it – naw! Naw!' he held out a hand, palm foremost, in Stacey's direction, as though to physically hold him off. 'You ain't thinkin' …?'

'Okay, okay! Take it easy. I ain't thinkin' nothin',' Stacey assured him. 'Jus' tell me what it is.'

'It's what I said, a crossbow. Like folks used to use in Europe, hundreds of years ago. I was tryin' to make one, jus' out of curiosity. Figgered it would be good for huntin' – I mean, no noise, you know? Wouldn' scare the game away. Jus' knocked this one together. I ain't even tried it out yet.'

'Show me how it works.'

Gregory nodded to the home-made weapon. 'It's jus' like a bow and arrow, only the bow lies sideways, horizontal like. An' it's a lot smaller. I made this one from a piece of an ol' road spring off a buggy.'

Stacey could see that. A piece of narrow, tensioned steel had been shaped like a bow – it measured about twenty inches across – and strung with thin wire cable. The bow had then been set crosswise across an old rifle stock, complete with trigger and guard. There was a groove for a bolt and a primitive sight.

'How do you work it?' Stacey tugged at the bow wire but it hardly yielded at all.

'Not like that. Lord! You'd never load it by hand. Too strong. Look!' Gregory lifted the wire-strung bow clear off the wooden stock. He inserted a metal tube between bow and string and began to unwind a smaller, screwed rod from within the tube. As the rod emerged with the winding it forced the wire back, bending the bow taut. When the bow was sufficiently bent, Gregory gingerly replaced it on the rifle stock, secured the wire bowstring over two trigger lugs, and carefully removed the expandable rod. 'There,' he breathed. 'All you gotta do now is put a bolt in.'

'Jesus!' swore Stacey. 'There must be a helluva tension in that thing. You got any bolts?'

'Jus' one,' said Gregory. 'It ain't very good eethur, but it's the best I could do.' He rummaged on the bench for a moment and brought out a piece of black iron bar, about six inches long and ground to a point at the end. A rough attempt had been made to affix stiff, feathered flights to the other end with wire bindings.

'You only got this one?'

'Yeah. Like I said, it's only an experiment. I ain't even tried it yet. Not once.'

Stacey pointed the weapon at a bale of hay that lay on the floor a couple of yards away. 'Is it safe?' His finger took up the trigger pressure.

'Yeah, I guess so. But I ain't never tried. ...'

There was a 'Whung' and a 'Thunk'. Stacey had squeezed too hard on the trigger. The hay bale jerked and he was left with the discharged weapon in his hands. Together they ran to the hay bale.

'I musta missed!' said Stacey in wonder. There was no sign of the bolt. He peered again at the load-less weapon.

'Naw, you didn' miss,' breathed Gregory. 'Goddam bolt's gone way inside this packed bale. Goddam near through to the other side.'

'An' not a sound,' whispered Stacey. 'Not a goddam sound. Load this thing again, Joe, quick.

I'll dig out the bolt.'

'You mean …? What you aimin' to do?'

'You know what, Joe. I told you already. I'm goin' into that store. I got to. I'm goin' to get clothes an' boots an' stuff, supplies.'

'Lord God of Hosts!' prayed Gregory. 'Guide us an' protect us.' He walked away a few paces then turned round and faced Stacey again. 'You ain't really thinkin' of goin' in there?'

'Joe, it's like I said. I got to get stuff. Only one place I can get it. An' there's a man in there, like you said. An' I can't use the gun. I got to try this. Ain't nothin' else I can do.'

'But that thing, it's only an experiment. We don't know how well it works. The sights might be faulty. You can't aim it from a distance. You'd have to get close. If you knew what he was like – the man in there – you wouldn't like bein' close to him. I mean, suppose things don't work out right? Ain't you scared?'

Stacey looked right into Gregory's eyes. His own face was chalk white, drawn and twitching. 'Joe, I'm shit-scared,' he confessed nakedly. 'But what in hell am I to do? An' I'll be close all right. That's what scares me most.'

EIGHT

They made their way to the window of the forge and stood there looking across to Lou Gans's store, a deep reluctance to go any further filling both of them like a gas.

'He's armed, you say?' asked Stacey unnecessarily.

'Yeah. Got two guns. An' even without guns he'd be. ...' Gregory shook his head. 'They ain't like us,' he concluded. 'They're a different kind of people.'

'When do you think would be the best time?' Stacey stalled.

They were distracted by sound coming up the street. They looked at each other, then peered out of the corner of the window to let themselves see further out.

Three women were coming up the street ... two older women and a young girl. The girl was carrying something in her two hands and she was weeping noisily. 'Mrs Miller and Mrs Gregg,' breathed Joe Gregory, 'an' Annie Slocum. What do they want? Where they goin'?' They watched attentively.

The women were heading for the store and it was plain that the girl didn't want to go with them. She dragged behind, half-turning back from time to time, wailing dismally and pleading with them constantly. The women too were upset but seemed resigned, even determined, to fulfil their intention.

'Aw please! Mrs Gregg. I don't want to go in there. Please don't make me. Please, please, please!' The words became audible to the two watching men.

'Now don't be silly, Annie.' Letty Gregg's voice sounded as if she was trying to be reasonable but was finding it very hard work. 'You know it's got to be done. An' nothin' goin' to happen. Just take in the fella's vittles, that's all. He won't hurt you none.'

'Jus' like Mrs Gregg says,' Lorna Miller tried to reinforce the other woman's assurance. 'You're makin' a fuss about nothin', nothin' at all. Man ain't gonna hurt ya. Jus' wants his dinner, is all ... an' somebody to talk to ... nice young gal ... while he's a-eatin' it. You'll be all right.'

'But you know what folks said,' pleaded Annie Slocum, her voice breaking, her pleading abject. 'He told them. An' I'm scared. I'm real scared. I'll do anythin' you want. Cookin', scrubbin', tendin' stock – I won't never complain. But don't make me go in there, with that man. ... You know what ...'

'Now that's enough, Annie Slocum,' Letty Gregg's tone was sharper now, more desperate. 'You know it's gotta be done, now. Gotta be! An' it ain't nothin', nothin' at all. You jus' gotta take the man's dinner in to him ... an' sit with him a little while, an' bring back the plates. An' we'll be waitin' jus' outside for ya. Waitin' right here. Ain't nothin' gonna happen to ya. Don't be silly now!'

'Mrs Gregg's right,' Lorna Miller remonstrated with equal energy. 'It ain't nothin', honest. An' remember what you owe to Mrs Gregg. Who's looked after ya all these years? Why, don't you think it's a mighty little thing to do for a woman who's taken care of ya all this time? When you had nothin' ... nor nobody ... to call your own. What about gratitude, girl?'

'Naw, naw ... please! Mrs Gregg!' The girl resisted desperately. 'I'll do anythin' – scrubbin', cookin' mendin' ... I'll wait on Betty, hand an' foot. Honest! Anythin', I'll do!' The women were opposite the forge now. The men could see that Annie Slocum carried a tray with food on it, though she was nearly dropping it in her distress. The other two women held her by the elbows and hustled her along. All were loud, noisy, distrait.

'Now don't be silly girl!' Lorna Miller insisted. 'Mrs Gregg jus' tol' ya, we'll be jus' out here waitin' for ya. Ain't nothin' gonna happen to ya with us out here now, is there?'

'You jus' take in the vittles,' urged Letty Gregg, 'an' sit with him till he's et. That's all. An' remember all I done for ya, like Lorna says. You gonna forget all I done?'

The door of the store burst open and Jack Holby stood there. Only for a second. Then he strode quickly forward and grabbed Annie Slocum by the arm. 'Well! 'Bout time!' he grinned. He shooed the

other two women away. 'Go on, beat it. You ain't
needed. C'mon, little girl. You an' me gonna have a
little fun.' He began to drag the crying girl towards
the open door. 'Ya heard me! Beat it!' he shouted
at the two hesitating women. They paused,
cowering, staring at Holby. He glared at them, his
fierce blue eyes blazing, thick tow-coloured hair
falling over his craggy forehead, mouth hanging
open, his huge form dwarfing the cringing girl.
'Aw, come on!' he snarled impatiently and dragged
the crying, struggling girl into the store, hauling
the door shut behind him. The two women stood
for a few seconds, staring at the door, then they
scuttled quickly away, their heads down and their
hands up round their ears, as though tryin' to shut
out sounds that they daren't allow themselves to
hear.

Stacey and Gregory gazed at each other
wide-eyed, saying nothing but understanding
everything. After a few seconds Gregory spoke.
'This is the time,' he said. 'Right now.'

'Yeah,' agreed Stacey, his voice a hoarse whisper,
his hands trembling visibly. 'I guess so ... when he's
occupied ... when he ain't thinkin'.'

They came cautiously out of the forge. There
was nobody in the street. It was almost as if nobody
wanted to be in the street, as if nobody wanted to
know what was happening. They crossed the dirt
road, side by side, crouching, and stood on the
boardwalk, right outside the store door.

They stopped there and looked at each other
again. There were indistinct sounds coming from

inside the store. Gregory's look was a question. Stacey nodded fearfully, the crossbow held in his shaking hands. Gregory pulled the door open noisily and they walked into the store.

Holby was down by the main counter. The tray of food had fallen to the floor and plates lay scattered around. He held the girl with one giant hand, pulling at her clothes with the other. She was naked from the waist up. Below was a pair of long, shabby drawers reaching to her knees. She was trying to keep these on, panting and whimpering, twisting and turning frantically. Holby was grinning hugely, his great bulk shifting around like that of a heavyweight boxer as he played with the girl. 'Yeah, you wanna struggle a little?' he grinned. 'Right! Right then!' He caught sight of the two men approaching. 'What the fug do you want?' His tone changed to one of anger. He shoved the girl to one side, still retaining hold of her with his enormous paw. The men were only half a dozen paces from him. He could see their terrified faces. 'You get your fuggin' asses out of here!' He flung the girl away from him in a surge of hot anger and dragging his Colt from its holster lunged towards the intruders.

Stacey hesitated a split second, torn between fear and outrage. He had never deliberately fired at a man in all his life ... and an image flashed through his mind of the iron bolt in the hay bale: he knew what this weapon could do. Then he saw the girl in the background – the long shabby drawers, the terrified face, the humiliation. And the forbidden memories of his own prison outrages came back to him: he saw again the grinning, evil faces surrounding him, felt the manacle chaining him to the wall, felt the overwhelming wave of terror. His eyes went again to the outraged girl. And he squeezed the trigger. There was a quiet, soft 'Twung!' and a faint whir of air.

Holby stopped as suddenly as a leaping dog brought up by a steel chain cemented to a stone wall. He stopped dead. For a couple of seconds he stood upright, unmoving, the Colt held level in his fist, then he fell to the floor like a felled tree, causing the whole building to shudder and dust to rise in a small cloud.

The two men stood looking down on him. Holby lay still, lifeless. Suddenly Gregory rushed to the window and peered out. The sound of the crash still echoed in their ears and dust hung in the air.

'Anybody around?' asked Stacey. 'Anybody hear anything?'

'Don't see nobody,' replied Gregory hoarsely. 'Nobody aroun' – yit, anyways.' Stacey stood just where he had been before, the discharged weapon still in his hands. Holby lay unmoving on the dusty floor, blood oozing around him in a widening stain. A sobbing, whimpering sound could be heard coming from somewhere in the store.

Stacey moved amongst the shelves and counters. 'Where are ya, ma'am?' he called quietly. 'It's okay now. We ain't gonna hurt ya, honest. It's Joe Gregory that's here now. You know Joe, don't ya? Joe ain't gonna hurt ya. You're safe now. You can come out ... git dressed.'

She was crouched under a small counter, her torn dress held before her protectively. She was shaking violently, tears still flowing down her dirty face. Stacey laid the crossbow down and squatted a little distance away from her.

'It's okay now, Annie,' he said quietly, using her name for the first time. 'Jus' you take your own time to come to. You're okay now. Nobody goin' to hurt you now.' He rose and searched among the goods laid out on the counter and found a blanket. He brought it to her. 'Put this aroun' ya, Annie,' he said. 'Cover yourself. You're gonna be all right.' She took the blanket gratefully, still whimpering, and covered herself.

Gregory was still watching at the window. He turned round, his face chalk white. 'What in hell do we do now?' he asked.

'Clothes, for me,' replied Stacey. 'Boots ... food. But first, this fella's Colt and shell-belt.' He went over to the body on the floor and quite deliberately took the pistol out of the dead hand.

His movements were different now, Gregory could see that plainly. His hands didn't shake. He turned the dead body over in a positive, detached manner and removed the shell-belt. His voice was different too: it was calmer, not near breaking point, as it had been before. Gregory realized this, but he could not understand why it should be so. He was puzzled.

'You say you only got one bolt for this crossbow thing?' Stacey handed the pistol and shell-belt to

Gregory. Gregory took it but simply held it in his hands, as though not knowing what to do with it. Stacey began to strip off his dirty, flapping prison clothing.

'Yeah. Jus' one. Why?' Gregory was severely shocked and frightened. Inside an hour he had been present at two violent killings. His nervous system threatened to collapse from shock.

'I thought we mighta been able to use that weapon again.' Stacey's voice was level, steady, controlled. 'It don't make no noise. That's good.'

'Use the same bolt.' Gregory didn't know how he got the words out. 'Take it from. ...' His eyes went to the dead body.

'Can't,' said Stacey. 'Remember how it went into that hay bale? Did the same thing with him. It's disappeared completely. Right inside him. We couldn't dig it out without. ...' He left the sentence unfinished.

Gregory dared to take a look. The bolt had struck Holby just under the ribs on his right side. There was a dark hole about three-quarters of an inch in diameter. There was nothing else; no exit wound; just a dark hole and a widening pool of warm, sticky blood. And a bad smell. Gregory threw up.

'Lord God! Look at you!' he spoke accusingly to Stacey, wiping his mouth. 'You've killed two men. You realize that? How can you jus'. ...' He broke off again in a new spasm of retching.

Stacey had torn off his awful prison clothes. He stood in the middle of the floor pulling a new pair of Balbriggans over his bare backside. He fastened the front buttons then stopped and looked at Gregory calmly. 'Yeah. That's right. I did,' he said. 'But don't worry about it: they woulda killed us. An' what about her?' He motioned towards the sound of the still sobbing girl. 'What about what he was gonna do to her?'

'But … you don't give a damn,' Gregory cried. 'You ain't even … upset! Jus' … jus'. … Well, it don't seem to bother you none. How can you. …'

Stacey was pulling on a pair of woollen socks. Again he paused and looked towards Gregory. 'Yeah. You're right.' He wiggled his feet appreciatively inside the socks. 'I'm different, somehow. When I hit that first fella – outside the forge – it was kinda … accidental, like – I mean I hadn't *thought* of doin' it, jus' had to do somethin', on the spur of the moment, so I done it. But him,' he looked towards the dead figure of Holby. 'I shot him. Deliberate. Saw what he was gonna do. Saw that girl's face. Saw cruelty … an' viciousness. … Saw misery … an' fear … an' shame an' sorrow an' humiliation. … An' I saw that I could stop that – if I shot him. So I shot him. An' I ain't sorry. Don't ask me to be. I ain't. Now where the hell am I to get a pair of pants?' He moved off and began to rummage around.

'Yeah? An' what are we gonna do now? That's two of their men killed. What happens now, eh?' Gregory demanded solutions, wanted everything made all right.

'What happens now is that I get clothes … boots … food. Then we go for number three.'

'Number three?' Gregory was incredulous. 'You ain't thinkin' ...?'

Stacey had found a pair of pants and was stepping into them. 'Yeah. I am. You said there was six of these fellas. An' one of 'em's sick. That made five. Two's dead now. That leaves three. One in the livery stable. He's next. I got to get my horses. An' we got a gun each now. Odds is gettin' better all the time.'

'Yeah. We got a gun each. But don't ask me to use mine.' Gregory laid his pistol and belt down on a counter. 'You know me, Dave. I ain't that kind. I ain't never shot at nobody. 'Sides, if we start shootin', them fellas will hear. There's still two of 'em fit to fight – an' they're different from you an' me – well, different from me, anyhow. Don't ask me, Dave, don't. I'm scared.'

Stacey was studying the other man. It was true: he was an unlikely ally. His round, childish face radiated fear and indecision. He was a good man – good blacksmith, good worker, kind man and imaginative creator, but not a fighting man. But then neither was *he*, Dave Stacey, a fighting man – or he hadn't been until a few minutes ago. But he felt different now. Why was that? He didn't know, but he suspected that it had something to do with *having* to be: you could do a lot of things if you were forced to do them.

'All right, Joe. I understand. I won't ask you to do no shootin'. An' in any case, you're right: they'd hear the shootin'. I don't want that yet. An' I got a way of dealing with the man in the stable, a quiet way.'

'How you gonna do that?'

'Leave it to me. But I'll need your help. Meantime, there is somethin' you can do for me. Go and find Edie. Don't tell her about him,' he nodded towards the body of Holby, 'or the fella in the forge. But tell her I'm here. That I'm tryin' to get all my stuff together ... gonna head west ... you know what I mean? Tell her I'll see her – when we've got rid of the other men. Will you do that for me?'

'Yeah.' Joe nodded, glad to be given such an undangerous task.

'Right then, you do that. I'll get the rest of what I need here. An' I'd better see to that girl, Annie.'

He got himself a shirt and put it on, then he went looking for a coat. Along the way he found a barrel of dried fruit and delved into it voraciously, cramming handfuls into his mouth as he searched around, clamouring for sugar. There was only water to drink but he helped himself copiously to that. Soon he had to stop eating and drinking, because even though he hadn't had enough to satisfy him, he realized that he had taken as much as his system could deal with: to take in more would have made him ill. He couldn't afford that: not with Krieg close behind him.

The girl Annie was still cowering in her hidey-hole. Stacey tried to quieten her.

'You're okay now, Annie,' he told her. 'There ain't no danger no more.' He hoped he wasn't being premature. 'Look, you better get yourself some proper clothes. Get what you need here. I'll square it with Lou Gans. I'm gonna leave him my stable, in payment, when I light out of here.' He saw that she was staring at him in some dread.

'Look,' he assured her, realizing her state of mind, 'I ain't with those fellas. Honest. I ain't got nothin' to do with them. I jus' come back home, is all. Jus' happened to come in when they was here. Honest, Annie, I tell ya, I ain't with them. I'm jus' Dave Stacey, who used to live here coupla years ago. An' I ain't done nothin' wrong, never, I promise ya.'

'You saved me ... from that man ...' Her words came out in a tremulous whisper.

'That's right. An' you *are* safe. So git yourself some proper clothes, whole outfit if you like. Like I said, I'll square it with Lou Gans. Anythin' else you need?'

The girl shook her head. Slowly she eased herself out of her hiding place, holding the blanket protectively in front of her. She looked skinny, plain, pathetic. She moved away a few paces then turned and looked back at Stacey. 'I don' wan't to go back to Mrs ... to Mrs Gregg,' she faltered. 'Can I stay here with you? For a while, anyways?'

Stacey thought for a moment. He didn't want her talking, didn't want folks knowing what was happening, not yet. 'Yeah, okay,' he told her. 'That might not be a bad idea. Now get yourself what you need ... an' see if you can rustle up some coffee. Jesus! What wouldn' I give for a real cup of coffee.'

The two men stopped at the creek to water their

horses, then remounted and took up their journey again, walking their mounts leisurely at first. There was a long silence between them, broken only by the creak of saddle leather and the thudding feet of the big steeldust and the chestnut as they plodded doggedly up the trail. Suddenly Holborn spoke.

'Say, why do you do this kinda work?' he asked, adding hurriedly, 'I mean you don't need the money. You tol' me so yourself. You got plenty – enough to start a ranch, or a different kinda life. You could have somethin' more ... well, permanent ... safer, too. Why this kinda work? Bounty huntin'?'

Krieg didn't look at him but kept his gaze on the trail ahead. 'An' I tol' ya it ain't *for* the money. I got a reputation to keep ... for always bringin' my man in.'

'Yeah? Well, you got your reputation. You could retire with that reputation intact. You don't have to keep on doin' it.'

Still Krieg didn't look at him. 'It's what I do – bring in criminals. They broke the law: I bring them in.'

'Yeah ... but some of 'em ... like the fella we're chasin' ... maybe they *didn'* break the law. Maybe they're innocent.'

'Courts say they've broken the law, that's good enough for me. I bring 'em in.'

'In other words, you don't care whether they're really guilty or not: you're gonna bring 'em in anyway ... an' have 'em put in places like that jail?'

Krieg gazed straight between the ears of the big steeldust as its head nodded and shook in its plodding gait up the endless trail. 'Now you got it,' he grunted. 'The position clear now?'

Holborn checked his chestnut momentarily and studied Krieg for a moment, a downright worried expression on his face. 'Ain't that kinda like playin' at bein' God? Decidin' who's done right an' wrong? Decidin' who should get punished?'

This time Krieg did look at him. He too checked his horse and turned his gaze directly on Holborn. 'I didn' say nothin' 'bout God.' He spoke very deliberately. 'Don' like to hear the Lord's name taken in vain. All I know is: they broke the law; they're on the run, an' I'm bringin' them back, like I do, every time. Me, Hal Krieg. That satisfy ya?'

'I don' know.' Holborn shook his head. He kneed his chestnut back into movement and recommenced the endless swaying in the saddle. 'I'd say there was somethin' else eatin' ya ... some kind of guilt or somethin' ... like you gotta take it out on some other poor bastard ... make *him* pay, in some kinda way.' He looked round to see Krieg's reaction but because of their positions and the fact that some ten yards separated them his words hadn't been quite audible to the other man. There was no reply, only the clump of hoofbeats, the creak of leather and the jingle of bit-chains. And Holborn let it go at that.

NINE

Max Slievan lay sprawled in a rough armchair in the parlour of Ben Partlin's house, his mouth lying open and his breath coming in congested snores as he slept the sleep of exhaustion: worry over his brother Abe and tension over keeping the town under control took their toll of him; his nights were largely sleepless and he could not avoid falling asleep from time to time during the day. For this reason he kept Johnny Reb with him most of the time. Johnny Reb, supposedly on guard, lolled in another chair, idly gazing out of the window.

In the other room, the bedroom, Ben Partlin and his wife hovered around the prone form of the man in the bed. They too were worried and drawn, the result of several days and nights of intolerable strain. Charlie Garside and Ann Morrow, the boy and girl hostages, slouched in chairs in opposite corners of the room. Time, the passage of three days, had greatly lessened their fear and, as is typical in the case of children, boredom had taken over. They sulked bad-temperedly in their respective corners, alternately grinning and sneering at each other.

'Any change, you think?' There was nothing bored about Sarah Partlin. A realistic woman, she knew when danger threatened and she knew that it didn't always have to be obvious. 'He don't move much, does he?' Her voice was a hoarse whisper.

'Don' know. He's always like that,' replied Ben, his lined face greatly aged in the last few days. 'He been like that all the time, since he came.'

'Lord, if only we could see some improvement,' sighed Sarah. 'Maybe, if he got well, they'd quit and leave, without too much trouble. What do you think it is, Ben?' She asked the question for the hundredth time.

Ben shook his head. 'I jus' don' know. Even if I did I wouldn' know what to do, but. ... You want to know what I think?'

Sarah nodded, her face at once hopeful and apprehensive.

'Well ... could be pneumonia. I mean it's like what Uncle Silas had, back in Abilene, years back.'

'Is that bad?'

Ben shook his head dolefully. 'Afraid so. Killed Uncle Silas. An' he had a doctor. Uncle Silas was jus' like him – jus' lay, not movin' much ... not eatin' nor drinkin' ... jus' lyin' there ... doin' nothin'. Hardly breathin'.'

Sarah shook her head and twisted her hands with worry. 'Lord! Lord!' she prayed. 'Help us through this trial.' She moved closer to the bed and peered at the still, silent man who lay there. 'Wouldn't do no good to try that liniment again?

Or maybe try to get him to drink somethin'?'

Ben too was consumed by anxiety. 'He's gotta eat ... or drink, at least. Man can't go on livin' 'thout drinkin'.'

'Mister! Mister! You hear me?' Sarah bent close over the unmoving form, her voice a low murmur. 'You oughta try to drink somethin'. We got some beef gravy here. Good nourishin' stuff – an' tasty too, real tasty. You oughta try it.' She eased the covers down from around Abe's neck and ears to allow him to hear better, and the sight of the pale face and wasted form stirred a reluctant compassion in her heart. 'You hear me mister?' she repeated, her voice softer, more tender. 'You really oughta try some of that beef gravy. You'd feel the better of it.' She ran her fingers into the damp hair in a spontaneous caress as she would have done in the case of a sick child. Suddenly she snatched her hand away in fright and horror. 'Lord Jesus Christ!' she swore uncharacteristically. 'The man's dead, Ben! The fella's dead!'

'What?' Ben jumped with fright. 'Naw! Naw! Don't say it Sairy! It jus' looks like that! He's awright! He always lies like that ... not movin'. ...'

'He's dead, Ben.' Sarah was more resigned now: the inevitable had happened, as she had feared it would. 'See for yourself. I know a dead man when I see one.'

'Lord Jesus! Lord Jesus save and preserve us!' Ben prayed. He edged towards the bed, shrinking with horror, and placed a hand on the forehead of the figure lying there. It was cold, stone cold and clammy. Ben left his hand there for a few seconds. There was no pulse, no 'tone' to the body, and Ben, too, knew; he too realized the awfulness of their position. The man was dead all right. Had probably been dead for a couple of hours.

'What in God's name do we do?' breathed Sarah, her eyes straying in the direction of the other room.

'I don' know … I jus' don' know,' breathed Ben. Then he became more businesslike. 'Don' say nothin' … yit,' he whispered. 'Cover 'im up again. Pull the covers up over his ears, like it was before … an' don't say nothin'. Give ourselves time to think.'

When he heard Gregory coming back, Stacey breathed deeply, preparing himself for a testing time. What did the future hold for him? Would Edie go with him? Would they actually get out of this nightmare? Find a new life? Actually escape from Krieg and … all that?

He hefted the gunbelt around his waist. He felt better now – well, anybody would, he figured, with food in his belly, and real clothes on his back. But the future? That was still uncertain, very uncertain.

He eased open the door for Gregory. 'You see her, Joe? What did she say? She go along with it?'

Gregory peered around him. 'Ever'thin' all right here?' he asked. 'The girl still around? Annie Slocum?'

'Yeah. She didn' want to leave – not yit, anyways. What did Edie say? Didja see her? Tell her?'

Gregory looked uncomfortable. 'Yeah. I saw her, Dave. But. …'

'But what?' Stacey was impatient. 'You tol' her I was here. ... That I didn' have nothin' to do with that business over at Windy Hollow? That I'm a-goin' west?'

'Yeah, yeah, I tol' her all that, but ... well ... look, Dave, it ain't my fault ... I mean ... well, Edie ... I tol' ya before, she kinda taken up with Lou Gans, since you been gone.'

'But I'm back now!' Stacey protested. 'An' I'm innocent. I'm goin' to make a new life. Things can be good again. You tol' her that?'

'Yeah, yeah. I tol' her. But. ...' Gregory struggled to express himself. 'Well, it's different, Dave. I mean, you been thinkin' like this for a long time ... these ideas have been reality to you. But Edie, she been livin' a different kinda life. ... She ain't been thinkin' like that. Maybe ain't been thinkin' of you at all. I mean you bein' away an' all like that. She been livin' a different kinda reality. An' now you're back ... well, she ain't sure. ...'

'Did she say she wouldn' go?'

'Naw. She didn' say that. Didn't say nothin', really. Jus' listened ... an' looked ... an' didn' say nothin'. But she was kinda shocked, like. Well, anybody would be, wouldn' they? Maybe it'll be okay when she gets used to the idea, Dave. Give her a little time.'

Stacey nodded worriedly. 'Yeah. Yeah, maybe you're right. Stands to reason she'd be shocked, like you say. Yeah, that'll be it, all right. She's jus' shocked. It'll be all right when I see her; when we're together. Yeah, it'll be awright then.'

'You're lookin' a whole lot better.' Gregory tried to change the conversation. 'With clothes an' all.'

'Yeah. Feelin' a bit better too. An' we still got things to do. What else is goin' on? Them other fellas still in their reg'lar places? One in the stable? Others in Ben Partlin's?'

'Far as I know, yeah.'

'Right. I'm gonna tackle the one in the stable now. Need your help.'

'I ain't gonna do no shootin', Dave. Like I tol' ya. ...' Gregory was quick to protest. 'You agreed. I ain't the type.'

'Ain't askin' ya to do none. Jus' want you to get that fella to come out to the livery-stable door, front door, that's all.'

'I can do that, I think. I'm supposed to be shoein' their horses. Can ask him about that. I guess he'll come out. What you got in mind? If you start shootin' them others will hear.'

'They won't hear nothin'. Now here's what I want you to do. First, I got to get up on to the roof of the stable. ...'

Buff Cammil wandered about idly inside the livery stable, bored and irritable. He glanced into the stalls at the horses standing there, turned away and half-heartedly studied a couple of saddles resting on pegs affixed to the walls, ambled back and cast a disinterested look out of the window into the deserted street. 'Fug!' he spat. 'This ain't no fun! That bastard Johnny Reb oughta be down here for a spell. I wanna get out there, see what's doin'. I'm goddam fed up with ...'

He stopped as he heard sounds from outside – the scrape of shod hoofs, clumping of horses' feet. He paused, listening.

'Hell! I don' know.' The voice was an indistinct murmur. 'Don' know which one ... One looks okay to me. Maybe I oughta. ... Naw, that won't do. Maybe ... Hell! They oughta tell a man. ...' There was the sound of horses moving, again the clink of horseshoe metal on stone. Cammil moved to the front door, with more interest than he had been showing for some time. Something was happening there; there was someone to look at, to talk to.

The blacksmith fella was there, just outside the door, with two horses, Maxie's and Mako's. The animals were unsaddled and the blacksmith was inspecting their feet. He was muttering and swearing quietly to himself as though he had some sort of problem. Apparently he didn't see Cammil.

'You got a problem?' Cammil's voice was mildly friendly. He felt friendly. The fact that he was part of a gang holding the town to ransom didn't make him feel unwelcome. The fact that he had brutally hacked down one of its citizens didn't, in his mind, prevent friendly relationships existing between himself and the townspeople. He leaned against the stable wall and watched with mild interest.

The blacksmith looked up. 'Yeah,' he said reluctantly. His face showed fear and Cammil felt pleased and gratified by that fact: he liked people to be afraid of him; it was a situation he understood.

'What's botherin' ya?'

The blacksmith shook his head. 'These horses. I don' know how much to do. Both need shod ... not all four feet, though. An' one of them got a problem foot. There's a coupla ways to treat that, but I don' know what the owner will ...'

'Shoe the goddam animals. You're a farrier, ain'tcha? You oughta know what to do. Ain't no good askin' Maxie. He don't know nothin' 'bout horses ... 'cept how to sit on one. Go on, shoe the critters.'

'Yeah, but. ...' The blacksmith hesitated, seemed unsure. He shook his head in perplexity. 'This could give him a lotta trouble.' He picked up one animal's near forefoot and studied it, hissing through his teeth and tut-tutting to himself. Up in the loft of the stable Stacey stood beside the windlass used for hoisting bales of hay up into the upper storey. He peered down. Cammil was too far back. He'd have to come forward six or seven feet. Stacey checked the rope of the windlass again: several feet of it lay ready uncoiled on the floor; it ended in the slip noose that they used for securing round hay-bales. All was ready. It would work – if Cammil could be brought forward a few feet.

'I don' figure I can do this job.' Joe Gregory dropped the animal's foot and wiped his hands on his leather apron. 'Animal maybe have to be destroyed.' He looked scaredly back to where Cammil lounged against the stable wall. 'Tain't my fault. Animal oughta been looked at earlier.'

'Aw, what the fug ya talkin' about?' Cammil

heaved himself off the wall with an exasperated sneer and wallowed forward towards the horses. 'They ain't fug-all wrong with that animal. Now if you was talkin' 'bout Holby's mount. ...'

He stopped, slightly confused, as something dropped over his head and settled around his thick neck, something quick and light, like a fly, almost. He brushed a heavy hand over his face and found a light rope around his neck. Before he could grasp it, either physically or mentally, it drew tight, choking off his wind. A sudden panic overcame him.

Up above, in the loft, Stacey held the rope taut with one hand and with the other swiftly wound the handle of the windlass until all the slack was taken up. Then he grabbed the windlass handle with both hands and began to wind, fiercely, hurriedly, with all his strength. Cammil was hauled clean off his feet, his thick legs and heavy, muddy boots wildly kickly the air. Down below, Joe Gregory ran away, unable to witness the spectacle.

Above, Dave Stacey thought of the man he had seen hacked down earlier that day, heard again the awful 'clunks' as the heavy bayonet cleaved down on his bare head, and he took another couple of turns on the windlass and secured the ratchet in place to keep the rope from unwinding.

Below, the heavy figure of Buff Cammil heaved and jerked in violent contortions. Choking, guttural noises sounded unheard on the quiet air. The woodwork of the stable creaked with the violence of movement. After a few minutes the struggles grew weaker, the woodwork creaked less frequently, the guttural noises ceased and finally the body of Buff Cammil swung lifeless in the afternoon air. Soon it even stopped swaying and just hung there motionless.

Johnny Reb strolled casually down the dirt street. It was good to get out of that house from time to time, even if just to check on the other fellas. It got stuffy in there ... kinda sick-like, with Abe lyin' there like that, so long too. You got fed up with it. An' Maxie warn't no good company – warn't good company at the best of times. He liked being with Cammil better, though Cammil was real dumb. He'd be glad when Abe got better. Then they could enjoy this town for a few hours. There were one or two good lookin' women aroun' – an' he hadn't had him a woman since ... goddam! He forgot! Musta been ... well, a long time. Too long. But Maxie wasn't havin' them crowd the women ... well, not yet. Not till Abe was better. Didn't want trouble from the menfolks. But surely Abe would get better soon? Then they could have their fun. If Abe didn't get better soon, well, Johnny was beginning to think about that. Maybe he'd take off on his own. Or with Cammil. They got along all right, Buff an' him. They didn't need Maxie or Abe. Could always join up with some other fellas. He turned his footsteps towards the stable. He'd look in on Cammil first, have a jaw with him. Then check on Mako and Holby.

*   *   *

Max Slievan stood gazing sullenly out of the window. Things weren't right, weren't going right, he could feel it. He liked to be in charge of things, calling the shots, and he wasn't doing that now, not right now.

He couldn't quite put his finger on it, but he knew – or he felt – that he wasn't in control. Aw, sure, he had this town under his thumb, for the present, anyhow – but nothin' was happening. They were just stuck here. Wasn't as if they were havin' a good time. Normally if they had descended on a small town like this they'd have made good use of it – fed themselves up real good, had a couple days good drinkin', screwed all of the eligible women, got it all out of their systems. Then they'd have fitted themselves up – fresh horses, new clothes, guns and ammunition, a good grubstake – and they'd have been away again, restored and healthy, satisfied and fresh for further travels. An' his men would have been satisfied with his leadership, would've been happy to fall into line.

But this! Hell, this wasn't no good to nobody.

What was wrong? He racked his limited brain in an attempt to understand the problem. Well, they had to lie low or account of Abe's sickness. Yeah, that was the trouble, Abe's sickness. He felt relieved to discover that the fault was not his own: it could've happened to anybody. And things could still be put right. When Abe got better they'd take possession of this town, enjoy themselves, get everything they wanted. Then his men would look up to him again. Things would be all right. When Abe got better. And it would be great to have Abe well again. He was worried about Abe, had been worried for a couple weeks. How was Abe doin' anyway? He hadn't looked in for a while.

'Hey, you fella!' he called out suddenly, heaving himself up from where he leaned against the wall. 'How the hell is that man doin'? You gettin' any results yit?' He hauled his heavy bulk towards the doorway to the bedroom. 'Lemme take a look at him.'

It was the woman he saw first. She turned towards him a face that was petrified with fright, lined, aged and past despair. Even then he didn't know, didn't realize. He made his way to the bed-head. The man, the little bald-headed, scared fella, stood in his way. It was clear that he was shit-scared, even more than usual, but he remained in Slievan's path, either deliberately or because he couldn't get out of the way. He even attempted to prevent Slievan reaching the bed-head. 'Don' wake him,' he pleaded, his voice shaking with fear, his limbs quaking visibly. 'He's sleepin'. Sleep's good for him … best thing for him … an' he et a little today … he's gonna be. …'

Slievan shoved him aside, suspecting nothing. Even the exaggerated shaking that he detected in Ben Partlin's limbs didn't register with him: men were usually afraid of him, especially nervy, scared little guys like this. He reached out a calloused

hand and with surprising gentleness drew back the
covers from Abe's neck and ears. 'Abe?' He spoke
as gently as he could. 'Abe? How you doin' son?
You hear me?' He reached into the bed coverings
and laid a hand on Abe's shoulder. 'How you
feelin', ol'-timer?' He gently shook the still
shoulder. 'Don't worry 'bout nothin', Abe. You're
gonna be all right. We got you to a medical fella.
You're in good han's. Abe? Can ya hear me, Abe?
Abe?' His hand trailed tenderly from the shoulder
up to the neck and he made to run his fingers
through the hair.

He stopped suddenly, frozen in the act. His eyes
bulged and his mouth sagged open. 'Abe!' he
croaked and he leaned heavily forward, shaking
the limp form, patting the cold, waxy face. 'Abe!'
The last word was a scream, a scream like a
woman's. 'You bastards!' he screeched. 'You
useless, rotten bastards! You let him fuggin' die!
He's fuggin' dead! Dead! Dead! Bastards!'

The big Colt was suddenly in his hand. Sarah
Partlin was out through the doorway, the girl, Ann
Morrow, pushed violently in front of her. Ben
Partlin was desperately trying to hustle the boy,
Charlie Garside, over to the doorway in an attempt
to get him out of the cabin. They were scurrying
like rats in a barn invaded by terriers. The Colt
boomed and flashed, again and again as Slievan
loosed off wildly in the general direction of the
fleeing people. Heavy slugs tore into the wooden
walls and floor. Ben Partlin went down in a crying,
crumbling heap in one corner, his body blocking

the escape of the terrified boy. Sarah Partlin and the girl surged out screaming into the street.

Johnny Reb saw the hanging body just a minute before he heard the shots. At first he thought that Cammil, dumb bastard, was playing some kind of game – but he only thought so for a moment: the hanging form was too still, too realistic. Reb ran forward a few incredulous paces then stopped again. It was no game: he saw the swollen, blackened face, the protruding tongue. Johnny Reb had seen one or two hanged men before; you couldn't fake it that good. Suddenly an unfamiliar stab of fear went through him and he turned and ran. Mako! was the thought that went through his mind. Get Mako! Then Holby. They're nearest. Then he heard the shots, several of them, coming from up the street. Things were happening, things were changing: he knew it. Maybe it was action at last? The unfamiliar fear went from him and his crazy grin came back on to his face. He reached the forge, heaved open the door.

Mako was lying on the ground, all tied up. He didn't seem to be moving ... face all bloody. There was more shooting, loud and violent. Johnny Reb didn't even wait or try to free the bound man. He turned and sprinted for the store. Holby would be there. Holby was bigger than Mako, tougher, a better ally. Get Holby first, then tell the boss!

He reached the store and burst through the door. The shooting had stopped, for the moment. The store was a mess, stuff lying scattered around everywhere. Holby was lying motionless in the middle of the floor. Now Johnny Reb knew that things were going wrong, badly wrong. 'Holby? Jack?' he called, throwing himself down and shaking the still figure. He knew in a second that Holby was stone cold dead, that his blood was soaking into him even as he knelt there beside him. He scrambled up from the floor and ran full tilt back towards the house, and Maxie and Abe.

TEN

'Boss! Boss! Holby's dead! An' Mako – an' Cammil – strung up! Cammil, I mean! They're dead, Maxie. All of 'em. We're on our own, Maxie!' Johnny Reb burst into the house, panting, his Colt drawn in his hand. He stared at his boss, the crazy grin fixed on his face.

'What? What?' Slievan stared at him, uncomprehending. His mouth hung open and there was an air of bewilderment about him, as though he had just woken up from a deep sleep. He too had his Colt in his hand and the room was filled with the stink of burned powder. The form of the little bald fella lay sprawled in a corner beneath a bloody splash on the wall. The boy hostage crouched gibbering in another corner. There was no sign of the woman or the girl.

Johnny Reb shoved the door closed behind him and checked the street. No one actually in the street but he could detect movement here and there between houses. They were coming out.

'They're dead, Maxie,' he repeated, barring the door with a chair. His movements were quick, nervous. He was keyed up, excited, after days of boredom. 'Holby an' Cammil an' Mako, all of them. These bastards been up to somethin', behind our backs.'

'They ain't the only ones.' Slievan was slowly regaining his senses, although he still moved sluggishily. 'Abe's dead. An' that li'l bastard!' He fired another deafening shot into the body sprawled on the floor and again the stink of powder filled the room. 'An' if it's killin' they want, well, they come to the right place. I don' give a fuggin' goddam' now. They want killin', I'll give em' all the killin' they got a belly for. I'll show the bastards ... lettin' Abe die ... fuggin' *killin'* Abe. They gonna find out 'bout killin' – the Maxie Slievan way.' He strode across the cabin and, grabbing the boy hostage by the shirt collar, hauled him to his feet. 'Let's see how they like a boy with no fuggin' head, to start off with.'

Johnny Reb watched him, showing neither fright nor horror. 'You gonna start on him?' he asked, the crazy grin seemingly fixed immovably on his young face. 'We gonna blast all of 'em? Gonna shoot it out here?'

'Yeah. They're gonna pay, the bastards. I made them an offer. The bastards double-crossed me. They're gonna suffer for that. But they're gonna *see* this li'l bastard get his fuggin' head blown off. Gonna see what they got comin' to them.' He dragged the gibbering boy towards the door. 'Now open that fuggin' door.'

Johnny Reb began to unbarricade the door then

stopped suddenly. 'Maybe they got guns?' He looked questioningly at his boss.

'They ain't. Didn' we take all the goddam weapons when we first came in?'

'Aw, yeah.' Johnny Reb turned again to the door then stopped again. 'Maybe they got Mako's gun? An' Holby's. An' Cammil's. They could be armed – well, some of 'em.'

'I tell ya I don' give a fuggin' goddam! They killed Abe. Now I'm gonna kill some of them. Open the fuggin' door, so that they see the killin' start.' He shoved the gibbering boy forward another couple of paces.

'But boss!' Johnny Reb, uncharacteristically, was having second thoughts. The sight of Cammil hanging high in the air was still vivid in his mind – the blackened face, the protruding tongue – and the cold body of Holby on the floor of the store, his blood congealing around him in a sticky glue. Holby ... an' Cammil ... an' Mako: it didn't take much imagination to realize that they were all going, one by one. Abe, too, was gone. Soon it would be Maxie's turn ... to be cold, and stiff ... or dangling on a rope in the warm afternoon air, choking and gasping for breath, his tongue filling his mouth, while people stood below and swore and jeered. Yeah ... it would be Maxie next ... or himself, Johnny Redbridges. Suddenly the awful reality of death swamped his mind. He could *see* himself dead – and in a few short minutes.

'Listen, boss.' He thought as quickly as he could, a difficult job for one totally unaccustomed to thinking. 'We can still get out … get away. We got the kid. Take him out, with a gun in his ear. We can get horses … an' grub. Get away. There's other places … we don' have to die … not right now. We can still have a lof of fun. Other towns … women, drink. … We can be on top again.'

'I already tol' ya! I jus' don' give a damn. I'm a standin' right here. You gotta go some time. I'm goin' with Abe. Got nothin' else to live for.' Max Slievan grabbed the boy hostage by the hair and shoved him forward. 'Open the fuggin' door!'

'Not this time, Maxie,' grinned Johnny Reb and squeezed the trigger of his Colt, shooting his boss through the body. Slievan jerked like a puppet on a string and his face showed complete bewilderment. He eased his grip on the boy's hair and the kid scurried away into a corner. Slievan's hand holding the Colt sagged downwards and the pistol dropped to the floor. Johnny Reb grinned and triggered off again, shooting his boss in the chest. Slievan crashed back against the wall of the cabin, his eyes showing the beginnings of realization, then quickly glazing over. So he stayed for a moment, held up by the wall, then he slumped lifeless to the ground.

Johnny Reb strode over and hauled the terrified boy to his feet. He dragged him over to the window. 'You out there!' he called. 'Hey! You people. Listen to me! I got this kid here. Can blow his head off if you like. But I'll make a deal with ya. Let me go an' I'll let him go. Jus' let me get a horse – good horse – some grub an' ammunition – an' you'll get the kid back unharmed. Hey you! Are you listenin'? I ain't gonna wait all day. Better think about it.'

There was movement out in the street, between the buildings; one or two men edged cautiously into the half-open, keeping close to the walls. They looked at each other, puzzled, uncertain. They had heard the shots and, though still afraid, they were curious.

'What is it?' asked one voice. 'Got any idea? What they up to now?'

'Don' know,' replied another. 'They say Sairy Partlin got out, with the girl too. But I ain't seen her.'

'Sairy out?' queried one man excitedly. 'You sure? How? Did they let her go? They quittin' or somethin'?'

Isaac Stone came cautiously out from between two buildings and joined the small group of men. 'Yeah, Sairy's out,' he confirmed. 'An' the girl too. But they still got Ben an' the boy in there. An' there's been shootin' – from in there, it seems. Don' know what ...'

The voice of Johnny Reb interrupted him. 'You hear me? It's me, Johnny Reb. I got the boy here. An' I can jus' as well blow his goddam head off. But I'm makin' ya a deal. Let me get a good horse – coupla horses – an' a grubstake n' some clothes an' ammunition ... an' I'll leave – an' I'll let the boy go, unharmed. I mean it. But I ain't gonna wait all day. Now let me hear from ya.'

The assembled men looked at each other. Isaac Stone called, 'What about the man? Ben Partlin. Our friend.'

'He's here. Wounded, I guess. But it warn't me who shot him. I ain't shot nobody – an' I ain't gonna, long as you get me that stuff, let me get away. But remember: I got the boy here. Now make up your goddam mind.'

Men and women, in increasing numbers, were joining the little group in the street and the news spread quickly. 'Sairy Partlin's out! An' the girl too.'

'Yeah, but Ben's shot. They shot him. Heard the shootin'.'

'Ain'tcha heard? One of 'em hanged himself! Down at the livery stable.'

'What? You kiddin'? Don't do to kid 'bout things like that!'

'It's true, I tell ya! Saw him myself. The big fat fella – one who chopped down Mike Connor. Musta been his conscience. Hung himself.'

There was an excited buzz of conversation accompanied by a woman's loud desperate wailing.

'That's Sairy Partlin now,' said someone. 'She jus' heard about Ben.' The wailing went on and on, the sound of someone maddened, inconsolable.

'They say they're tryin' to make a deal. Want horses an' stuff. Then they'll go.'

'Why they gonna do that? Is the man better? The sick man?'

'Naw. They say he's dead. Now they're tryin' to make a deal. Want horses an' stuff. Then they'll go.'

A boy came running madly down to join the group, running without any caution, desperate to break the news.

'Lou Gans is back in his store – an' there's a dead

man in there! On the floor. Lyin' in a pool of blood. Been shot, Lou thinks!'

The flurry of speculation increased. Everyone was talking at once. And the mood of the people was changing: three of the gang dead meant that there were only three left. The odds were changing. Courage, previously in short supply, was coming back to the inhabitants of Blake's Canyon.

'Don' make no deal,' called Tom Morrow. His hand went inside his vest to the pistol stuck in his waistband, the pistol he had taken from the dead body of Cammil as it swung in the air. The feel of it gave him a strange new courage. 'They don't deserve no mercy. We oughta string 'em all up!'

'You can talk!' shouted Ed Garside. 'They still got my boy in there. Let 'em go, I say. Save my boy. That's all that matters.'

There was a chorus of voices.

'Yeah. We gotta think of that.'

'That's right. They still got the boy.'

'We don' want no more killin'.'

The voice of Johnny Reb came again. 'How long you gonna wait? I tol' ya. I'm on the level. Get me a coupla horses an' some grub an' ammunition an' I'll let the boy go. Long as you let me get away. Boy won't come to no harm, I promise ya. Now what's it to be? 'Cause I can jus' as easily blow the kid's fuggin' head off. I ain't got nothin' to lose.'

'He keeps saying' "I".' Luke Brenner laid his hand on Isaac Stone's arm and looked carefully at him. 'He don't say "we". You reckon he's on his own? Could it be that there's more of 'em dead? We dealin' with jus' one man?'

The buzz of speculation surged even more loudly when this idea reached the ears of the crowd. Another one dead, perhaps? Now they felt they were getting the upper hand. The idea of a deal seemed less attractive than before.

'I say we ought to string 'em up,' Tom Morrow called again. 'Every last one of 'em. They don't deserve no better.'

In what had formerly been his own home, Dave Stacey was confronting his wife.

'I tell you again, Edie, an' I can't be no more truthful: I didn' have nothin' to do with that business over at Windy Hollow. But I'm on the run. I got to get away. Because they're after me – well, one man is – an' he don't give up. I got to get far away. Way west of here. We'll be okay there. …'

His wife was reluctant to look him in the eye. 'Yeah. I believe you,' she said unconvincingly. 'But I don' know, Dave. I mean, you say they're after you … an' they don't give up. What happens when they catch you? What about me? What happens to me? Way out there, miles from anyplace. I mean here I know people. It ain't fair to expect me to …'

'Edie, you married me,' Stacey pointed out. 'Don' you remember the words of the service? For better or for worse? I mean a wife oughta go with her husband. An' we'll be okay, I tell ya. We'll meet other folks, new friends. An' I'll work hard, Edie, I promise ya. I'll *be* somethin' … amount to somethin'.'

'Yeah?' There was something like a sneer in Edie Stacey's voice. 'An' jus' how you gonna do that? It didn' happen in five years of marriage. What makes you think it's gonna happen now? An' out there too ... place you're figgerin' on going ... what makes you think it'll be any easier there?'

Stacey shook his head. 'I don' know, Edie,' he said miserably. 'I don' know. I can't guarantee nothin'. But I'll work, Edie, work like a horse. I ain't afraid of that, Edie, you know that's true. I promise ya, Edie. ...'

'Promises?' his wife retorted indignantly. 'Promises? Yeah, you was always the one for makin' promises! Trouble was they never came to nothin'. An' anyway, how can you promise a woman anythin'? You can't even promise you won't go back to jail!'

'Aw, yeah!' Stacey suddenly grabbed her by the upper arms and held her facing him. 'Aw, yeah! That's one promise I can make – an' one I can keep: I ain't goin' back to jail. I don' care where I go, or who goes with me, but I ain't goin' back to jail, even if I have to run to the furthest corner of this country. Now are you gonna come with me? I ain't got a lot of time. Gotta move on soon. You comin' or not?'

'Heh! Let go of me, willya!' His wife broke away. She moved away quickly to stand by the window, her back to her husband. She looked up the street to Lou Gans's store. A small crowd, about half a dozen people were standing outside the building. If she, Edie Stacey was going to establish herself with Lou she'd have to do it now: the years were passing and time wasn't on her side.

'Naw. Sorry, Dave.' She turned and faced him, her mind made up. 'I ain't leavin' here. I ain't goin' to no new place. 'Tain't fair to ask me ... an' you on the run an' all. 'Tain't fair to a woman. A woman got a right to a decent future. An' you know it's true – they'll take you back to jail, sooner or later. I don' want to depress you Dave but ...'

'But Edie! I'm your husban'! An' I promise you, it'll be all right, when we get away. Edie! Please! Think about ...'

'I said I'm sorry, Dave!' She cut him short, angrily. 'But it's over – you an' me. You been away too long. A woman got a right to a life of her own. I'm stayin' right here.'

'But Edie ...!'

'Forget it, Dave! D'incha hear me! I said it's over. If you're goin' you'd better go. I ain't goin' noplace with you! You understand? Noplace!'

ELEVEN

Isaac Stone stepped with great care out into the open. His legs trembled and he expected to be shot at any moment.

'You in there!' he called loudly. 'Fella who wants to make a deal. We'll take your offer. We'll git you two horses – an' a grubstake, an' some ammunition – an' we'll let you ride out, in safety, if you'll send out the boy, right now.'

'Get the horses,' called Johnny Reb. 'Bring 'em up here, saddled. Put a pack-saddle on one, with the gun an' the ammunition on it. An' stand back – well back. I'll bring the kid out. Gonna take him with me for a coupla miles – but he won't come to no harm. Promise ya I'll let him go, soon as I get clear away.'

'Naw, naw! Don't accept that,' called Tom Morrow. 'That ain't no deal. How do we know he'll keep his word? He might still shoot the boy.' His hand went to his belt again.

The feel of the cold butt in his hand and the knowledge that he was the only man there with a gun reassured him. 'I say we don't make no deal,' he protested loudly. 'They don't deserve no mercy, after what they done.'

An excited babble followed this remark:

'Tom's right. They don't deserve no mercy.'

'Naw! Be sensible. We got to think of the boy!'

'How do we know he'll keep his word? They're bad enough to kill the boy, once they get away. Don't make no deals, I say.'

'Lord Jesus! We *got* to make a deal.' It was the anguished voice of Ed Garside. 'How'd you feel if it was your boy in there? Isaac? Mr Stone? Ain't I right?'

All eyes were turned in Isaac Stone's direction. The tall, grizzled man thought hard for a moment. 'I been thinkin',' he said. 'It's true – we let him go, he might kill the boy anyway. On the other han', we try to force him out of there an' there's a good chance he *will* kill him. Seems to be the bes' thing would be to let him go, an' take a chance that he'll keep his word an' let the boy go unharmed.'

There was a mumble of undecided voices but the voice of Luke Brenner was clear and strong. 'You're right, Isaac. That makes sense. Thank the Lord for your good sense.'

Isaac took a couple of wary steps further forward. 'You in there!' he called. 'Mister ... whatever your name is. We'll make that deal. Gonna send for the horses now – an' the other stuff too. But don' harm that boy. We won't spare you if anythin' happens to that boy.'

'You got nothin' to worry 'bout.' The voice of Johnny Reb came back. 'Jus' keep your side of the bargain.'

Isaac turned to a bystander. 'Go down to the livery stable,' he instructed him. 'Saddle a couple of decent horses – their own horses, ones they rode in on. An' explain to Lou Gans. Tell him we'll need a grubstake an' some ammunition. He won't lose by it, tell him. I'll see that he gets paid, somehow.'

The man ran off, accompanied by a couple more who were anxious to be in on the act. The others waited, standing idly around and talking excitedly amongst themselves. Tom Morrow was especially active, walking from group to group, his hand on the hidden Colt in his belt.

'I don' like it,' he protested. 'Shouldn' make no deals with scum like that. Like shakin' han's with the devil, you ask me. They oughta be strung up or shot dead, after what they done here.'

There were subdued murmurings.

'Yeah, guess you're right, but what else can we do?'

'Reckon Isaac knows what he's doin'.'

'He got a good head on him, Isaac Stone. Best do like he says.'

In twenty minutes the messenger was back along with his voluntary escort. They led two horses, one bearing a riding saddle, the other a pack saddle loaded with stuff. They led them out into the open, into plain view.

'All right, mister!' called Isaac Stone. 'Here's your horses. Grubstake too ... an' ammunition, like you asked for. You can go – but remember what we said 'bout that boy.'

'Now you all stand back, well back,' called Johnny Reb. 'I'm a-comin' out. But don' try nothin', 'cause I got the kid, remember!'

'Stand back men,' called Isaac Stone. 'Right back now. Remember the deal we made. Things gonna be all right, in a little while, you'll see. Stand back now.'

The little crowd of men and women shuffled back reluctantly then stood and watched with great curiosity. How many people would come out of that ill-fated cabin? What condition would they be in? Would the boy be all right? How was he bearing up?

There was an audible creaking and the cabin door eased slightly open. A pause, then it opened a little further. They could see the crouching, shivering form of Charlie Garside and behind him, with one hand on his shoulder, one of the outlaws. They waited, expecting more.

The boy was shoved forward a few paces, the man right at his back. The cabin door remained open. No one else appeared. There was just one of them, after all.

Johnny Reb forced the blundering boy forward just over the threshold. He kept one hand on the boy's shoulder. In his other hand he held a Colt. They shuffled forward a couple of awkward paces.

Suddenly there was a pistol shot – from the crowd – a totally unexpected, ear-splitting bang! Johnny Reb jumped like a shot deer then frantically, awkwardly hauled himself and the boy back inside the cabin and slammed shut the door.

'Bastards! Bastards! Bastards!' he screamed. 'You want to play rough? You want to play dirty? All right then! You done it now! How 'bout this then?' There followed another deafening gunshot, then another and another.

There was consternation among the collected townspeople.

'Who the hell shot at him?'

'What the hell's goin' on? Who was shootin'?'

'Has he shot the boy? Isaac warned this would happen.'

'Who in God's name shot at him? That warn't the deal we made.'

'Was Tom Morrow here!' came one voice. 'Standin' right beside me. Got a Colt. Where'd you get that? You know you shouldn' a. ...'

Morrow was standing looking foolishly defensive and guilty and downright frightened. 'I didn' mean ... I thought ... I mean I didn' mean to shoot ... gun jus' kinda went off in my han'.'

'That ain't true, Tom, an' you know it! You brought up that Colt and levelled it at him. Saw you do it. Couldn' believe my own eyes!'

'Well, you done it now, Tom Morrow. You got the boy killed, mos' like.'

There was a sudden commotion, a heaving, scattering in the crowd and Ed Garside threw himself at Morrow. 'You goddam bastard!' he swore. 'You got my boy killed! I'll kill you for that.'

'Hold on! Hold on!' Isaac Stone forced himself between the two men. 'We don' know the boy's dead yet. Might be still alive. We just heard shots.

Wouldn' make no sense for him to shoot the boy, even now. He might be still alive.'

Several men held Ed Garside. 'Isaac's right,' they insisted. 'Don' do nothin' desperate yit. Your boy might be still all right.' Others grabbed hold of Morrow. 'Give us that goddam gun! Goddam fool! Ain'tcha got no more sense? Now you spoilt the whole thing. That fella ain't gonna come out now. How in hell we gonna deal with him now?'

Morrow, shamefaced and minus his treasured Colt, slunk to the back of the crowd and fell uncharacteristically silent. Isaac Stone was thinking again and shaking his head.

'He won't come out again, easy,' he sighed. 'Gonna take a long time. We're gonna have to reassure him that it's okay. That's gonna take time. Why in ...' he suppressed a curse word, 'did that fella have to shoot? We're jus' gonna have to wait, I guess.'

'Isaac, we can't wait.' It was Ed Garside. He wasn't asking this time: he was stating a fact. 'My boy's in there. Maybe wounded, maybe dyin'. I ain't waitin'. Don' care what it costs, me nor anybody else: I ain't waitin'.'

'Ed's right, Isaac,' another voice called. 'An' it ain't jus' the boy. Remember, Ben Partlin been shot too. Maybe Ben's lyin' wounded in there too. Time ain't on our side. We gotta do somethin'. Get that fella outa there. There ain't only but one of 'em left, seems like.'

Isaac nodded. 'I guess you're right. But what can we do? Anybody got any ideas?'

Ash Kozak pushed himself eagerly forward. '*Smoke* him out, Isaac! It'll work. Used it myself, once or twice, with bees, once – an' one time with a vicious dog. It works, I tell ya. Nearly choked myself to death that time. I tell ya it'll work all right. I can make up the smoke pack. Put it under the cabin an' light it. Bring him out in ten-fifteen minutes, I guarantee it.'

Isaac Stone nodded. 'It's worth a try, I guess. Can't think of nothin' else, anyways. Go an' get your smoke pack, Ash.'

In another fifteen minutes Kozak was back, a flat, bulky package in his hands, wrapped in sacking. 'Sulphur, coal oil, animal fat, sawdust,' he explained. 'Jus' get it under the floorboards, light it. It'll bring him out all right.'

'Yeah, but what about the boy? An' Ben Partlin'?' someone called. 'They're in there too. What about them?'

'I don't think it'll harm them too much – long as the fella don't stay in there too long,' explained Isaac Stone. 'Anyways, we don't have any choice. But we got to get it under the floorboards. Who's gonna go up there and place it in position an' light it?'

There was a long and very awkward silence. Gradually a few murmurings were heard.

'Gonna be dangerous, goin' up there. He's liable to take a shot at you.'

'That's right. An' he got a clear field of fire. Can see you comin' plain as day.'

'I'd go myself,' said Isaac, truthfully. 'But I don'

move good, an' that's a fact. Got arthritis. Can't stoop none, an' can only move slow an' awkward. I'd be askin' to get shot.'

'Why not ask Tom Morrow to go an' place it?' called a voice. 'It's his fault that they're back in there. He oughta go.'

A lot of people turned and looked at Morrow.

'I couldn', honest,' he mumbled, shamefaced. 'I got a bad leg.' This fact had been totally unknown till now. 'Like Isaac. Can't walk too good. Got it breakin' a horse, years ago, long time before I came here. I'd do it, if I could but I can't ... honest. Got a bad leg. ...'

'Well, somebody got to put it under the cabin,' repeated Ash Kozak. 'It'll work all right, if it's put in the right position. But somebody got to go right up close ... an' we ain't got all day.'

He stopped abruptly as the package was taken brusquely from his hands. He turned and saw Dave Stacey walking away with the smoke pack. 'What ...? Who ...?'

Stacey, unexpected, and in strange new clothes was not recognized at first. And the crowd, mesmerized by the threat of danger, and a possible killing, watched silently as he suddenly sprinted, zig-zagging, towards the cabin.

A shot rang out – and another and another. Dust spurted up from close to Stacey's running feet but he ran on, bent nearly double and zig-zagging wildly. He reached the cabin and flung himself down on the ground. The crowd could hear more shots. The man inside was firing somehow, at something, they couldn't know what. They waited, almost choking with apprehension and curiosity. Smoke began to spiral into the air, a thin, lazy column, and after a few minutes Stacey rolled away from the cabin, scrambled to his feet and began running back, again bent nearly double and zig-zagging furiously. Again dust spurted close by him as more shots came from the cabin. He was almost back to the safety of the crowd when he was hit. He sprawled headlong, then hauled himself painfully to his feet again and began scrambling towards safety. More shots sounded and inarticulate, half-heard curses from the man inside the cabin, then Stacey reached the fringes of the crowd and collapsed in a heap. Immediately he was surrounded by anxious and curious admirers.

'Who is he? Where'd he come from?'

'He hit bad? Where'd he get it?'

'You did right bravely, mister! Make all of us feel right small.'

'Jesus Christ!' Two or three voices at once. 'It's Dave Stacey!'

Fifteen minutes passed. The attention of the crowd was divided between the astonishing appearance of Stacey wounded in the arm, and the thick smoke that was billowing from the cabin. The air was filled with the babble of excited voices. Suddenly a cry went up. 'He's comin' out!'

It was true. The cabin door creaked open and Johnny Reb came out, alone. He held his Colt in one hand and wiped unceasingly at his eyes with the other. His head was bent and he staggered, like a man half-suffocated. He seemed in danger of falling down.

'Don' shoot!' he gasped. 'I surrender. I give up! The kid ain't hurt. I didn' shoot him. Shot into the floor. Jus' let me breathe. You can have the kid. Jus' let me go is all. Let me get my horse.'

He peered through red-rimmed, weeping eyes in the direction of the two saddled horses and staggered towards them. The crowd watched, an uncertain, unstable crowd. They moved closer to the staggering man, partly through curiosity, partly unknowingly. They moved closer still, slowly but definitely. The gap between them narrowed dangerously.

Johnny Reb didn't notice. He couldn't see properly, was concentrating on reaching the horses, couldn't walk right. A number of women were to the forefront of the crowd.

Johnny Reb reached his horse, his own horse. He recognized Maxie's horse alongside it, with a pack-saddle on. He began to mount and found the Colt in his hand an awkward hindrance. Unsteadily he tried to holster the weapon but missed the holster. The weapon clattered to the hard earth. Johnny Reb looked down, tried to decide whether to stoop and retrieve the weapon. Swiftly, in a sudden panic, he decided not to and tried to grab the saddle horn. There was a sudden rush of movement-noise and a savage surge of bodies towards him. A fierce wave of people swamped over him.

The women were first, about a dozen of them. They tore Johnny Reb from his horse as he tried to get into the saddle. He screamed and struggled madly, all arms and legs flailing the air but they dragged him to the ground, clawing, tearing, gouging, fighting viciously with each other to get at him, to rend him, to destroy him.

Unbelievably, he got up and, using all his young strength, tore himself free and tried to run away from them. For a few seconds it looked as if he might actually get away. He gained a few yards, scrabbling frantically and casting wide-eyed glances back at them, his crazy grin incredibly still on his ashen face, then there was a shot and he went down in a clatter of bones, his spine shattered by a slug from his own Colt. Kate Connor stood awkwardly holding in two hands the Colt, which she had clawed up from the ground where he had dropped it. She tried to shoot him again as he lay there but she was too inexpert and couldn't work the weapon more than once.

There was no need, anyway. The crowd didn't wait. They were on him in a sudden surge, a hate-maddened swarm, like a pack of vicious dogs. This time he didn't get up. Couldn't get up. They fell on him and rent him asunder, men and women both, the anger, fury and hate of four terrible days filling their minds and souls. They kicked him and tore at him, hammered and flailed at his squirming body, men's boots and women's talons fighting for an opportunity to wound him, destroy him. Their hands and faces became bloody, his clothes turned to rags, his struggling body to limp carrion, cooling quickly as the last vestiges of life left it.

There was little left of him when they had finished. Then they went rampaging through the town, seeking other targets for their rage. They found only Mako alive and they fell on him.

Later, they were exhausted, dazed, moving like sleepwalkers. Bloody and horrified, they could not bear to permit themselves the realization of what they had done, of what they themselves had, even temporarily, become.

TWELVE

Hours after the last slaying, the town of Blake's Canyon was still in a turmoil. People wandered about, bewildered, hardly aware of themselves or of what they had done or had still to do. No one knew anything for sure: rumours were rife and a vast confusion swamped everything.

Groups of people stood in the street, arguing and contradicting and in half a dozen houses impromptu meetings were taking place.

Isaac Stone was having problems. Standing leaning against the wall in Ash Kozak's cabin surrounded by noisy, excited townspeople all talking at once, he was finding himself pulled in every direction by the competing claims of people with different attitudes towards Dave Stacey.

'He ain't no better than them we jus' threw out!' expostulated Reuben Watts. 'Jus' the same type. Criminal. Rapist, by God! He got to leave, right away. We don' want his type here.'

'He ain't figgerin' on stayin',' Joe Gregory put in timidly. 'Figgers on leavin', soon as he can. He don' want to stay here.'

'Good riddance!' called another man. 'Let him go. We ain't got no problem then.'

''Jus' wants a few things,' added Joe Gregory. 'Then he'll be gone.'

'We don' owe him nothin',' called Watts. 'Let him leave. …'

'Now hold on, Reuben!' protested old Caleb Grieve from a far corner of the room. 'Maybe we do owe him somethin' … quite a lot in fact. Joe here says it was him who got rid of them … murderers.'

'It was, too,' nodded Joe. 'He …'

'How the hell do you know?' called Doug Lambert. 'We killed a couple of them ourselves.'

'I tell you I know,' shouted Gregory, with uncharacteristic warmth. 'I was with him, goddammit! I tell you I *saw* him kill the fella in the store. An' the big fat fella in the stable. I *saw* him I tellya!'

'Well, that kinda proves it,' argued Reuben Watts. 'He's the criminal type. Thinks nothin' of killin' people. Takes a special type to act like that.'

'I'd be careful what you say 'bout that, Reuben,' called old Caleb from his corner. 'Lot of people aroun' here today with blood on their han's. I ain't sayin' I blame 'em but well, don't seem right to condemn a man for doin' somethin' that you done yourself.'

There was a short, awkward silence and a number of people actually looked down at their hands. Isaac Stone took the opportunity to take control of the meeting.

'Well, I'd say we give Dave the things he wants – if he means to leave us – an' let him go. I guess he did get rid of most of that gang for us. Joe here saw him do it, an' Joe don't lie.' Gregory nodded in grateful appreciation.

'Yeah, but they say the law is after him,' called another man. 'What do we tell them, when they come here? I mean, if we don' say nothin', well, we're kinda helpin' a criminal to escape. An' that ain't right.'

'Well.' Isaac Stone heaved himself off the wall and leaned forward to make his point. He spoke not just to the speaker but to all the people assembled there. 'I repeat what I jus' said: I say we let him go, an' say nothin' to nobody. Don' matter what you think of Dave Stacey, fact is you an' me might be dead right now if it wasn't for him. Stone, stiff dead – like them corpses laid out behind the stable – you an' me. Way I see it, that means we owe Dave Stacey our lives. Be a poor way to pay him back if we was to make any kinda trouble for him. I say we give him what he wants an' let him go – an' we don' say nothin' to nobody.'

There was a low rumble of voices, discussing, objecting, reaffirming, but the mood of the meeting was resolved: they'd do what Isaac recommended: he was a man of standing in the community, a man who often made decisions for them – and as for them, they were very ordinary people, who hated nothing so much as having to make decisions for themselves.

Joe Gregory quietly extricated himself from the meeting and made his way down to Stacey's own home. Here he found Stacey alone, sitting amongst some collected belongings. He was dressing his arm wound. His galled wrist too was bare; raw and sore-looking.

'Is it bad, Dave?' began Gregory. 'The arm, I mean. You hit bad?'

'Bad enough,' replied Stacey with a tight, wry grin. 'But there ain't no bones broke, thank the Lord. Won't stop me ridin'.'

'You can't do that yourself,' said Gregory, experiencing a sad compassion as he watched the sore, lonely man trying awkwardly to administer to his own wounds. 'Here, lemme help ya. Ain't your wife aroun'?' He took the bandage from Stacey and began to dress the wound.

'Naw. She's out somewhere. Gone to the store, I think. Got some supplies to get, I guess.'

'I jus' come from a meetin',' explained Gregory. 'With Isaac Stone an' them. They appreciate what you done, Dave.' Gregory hoped he wasn't stretching the truth too far. 'Gonna let you get your stuff an' go. An' they ain't gonna say nothin' to nobody – I mean to the fellas that's followin' you.'

Stacey once again gave the tight grin. 'That's fine, Joe. I ain't askin' no more'n that. But Joe, I got to ask you a favour.'

'Jus' ask, Dave. I guess I warn't much good to you – dealin' with them … fellas … I mean – but I'll do what I can for ya. I know how much we owe you.'

'Well, it's a fact that some people are after me. One man in particular, an' he don' never give up. He mus' be close behin' me … maybe coupla days, maybe more, maybe less. An' I can't go jus' yet, Joe. Gotta get my stuff together. An' I need some sleep too, an' some cooked food. Gotta have a little time to ... well, kinda get myself together.'

'I understan',' nodded Gregory, then added spontaneously, 'I'll miss you, Dave. Be sorry to see you go.' He meant it sincerely. 'What do you want me to do?'

'You know Temple Rock?'

Gregory nodded. It was a well-known landmark. A high rocky bluff that commanded a view for miles around.

'Would you go there? Watch the trail for a few hours? You can see the trail for miles from there. You could see anybody comin' long way off. I could get some rest, get things organized – an' know that nobody was sneakin' up on me. Soon's I'm ready, I'll ride out. Would you do that, Joe?'

'Sure Dave. Be glad to. You rest easy a while. I'll let you know if anybody comes. An' about horses, when you go, why don' you take them dead men's horses? There's three of them that's good, an' I've already shod them. They're better than them animals of yours, Dave. An' I got an' ol' pack-saddle you can have. Want me to get them ready?'

Stacey looked at him. It was the first time in a long while that anyone had offered to do anything for him. His voice was husky. 'Thanks, Joe. I'd appreciate that. That'd be jus' fine.'

There was a knock at the door and it was pushed tentatively open. Old Caleb Grieve stood there, leaning on his stick, fat Bea Gunther at his side holding a steaming bowl. 'Dave?' Caleb's voice was old, quavery. 'Heard you was here. Might need a little help. Want you to come over to my place. You can lie down there a while and won't nobody bother you, I'll see to that.'

'An' I got some stew for you,' added Bea. 'Best of stuff, too. An' some bread. Do you good. I'll bring it along to Caleb's. We want you to know we appreciate what you done.'

Stacey looked up. His lips twisted in a little smile but when he spoke his voice was husky and his eyes misted over strangely. 'That's mighty kind of you Bea, Caleb. I'd like that fine. Ain't nothin' I'd like better.'

It took the town several hours more to settle. The excitement was a long time in dying down. Lou Gans was all over town, looking for lost stock. He had already stripped the stolen clothing from the dead bodies that lay behind the livery stable. People kept going round there to stare at the bodies. A man was positioned there to keep kids away. All in all it was a long time before the town reassumed anything like normality.

Attitudes towards Stacey continued to be mixed too and when, in the early evening, he came out to his three horses, ready, waiting and saddled, a small crowd had collected. Their faces reflected mixed emotions – relief, hostility, pity, shame and general discomfort. There were subdued mur-murings but little direct comment.

Stacey began to load his belongings on to the

pack-saddle – clothes, food, an axe, one or two pots and pans. He was wearing the Colt that he had taken from Mako. He went back inside and came out with more stuff – blankets, more tools, some ammunition for the Colt, a spare shell-belt, a waterproof slicker. He loaded them on to the pack horse. The two riding horses were those that had formerly belonged to Maxie Slievan and Mako, a big heavy dark bay and a sorrel. Mako's sorrel carried a rifle in a rifle boot. The pack horse was Johnny Reb's. As Stacey on strapped the load he kept looking into the small crowd, searching for his wife. At first he could not see her but after a while she appeared, keeping in the middle of the crowd, not getting too near the front.

Stacey did not seem to be in a hurry. On the contrary, he seemed to be putting off time, as if hoping something might happen that would affect his leaving. Joe Gregory rode in with the news that the trail was clear: there was no sign of anyone approaching the town. Still Stacey seemed reluctant to leave. Eventually, however, he could pretend no longer. He tightened the last knots, moved from the pack horse to his mount and took up the reins. He looked into the crowd, searched the faces for a moment and found his wife's.

'Well ... I'm a-goin', Edie.' He tried to make his voice strong, matter-of-fact, but it betrayed tension – fear, almost. 'I won't be back this way, I guess, ever. If you've had any second thoughts ... I mean, if you've changed your mind ... I'd still like for you to come along.' He paused awkwardly, reluctant to display his personal affairs openly before so many people. 'I meant what I said, Edie. Didn' have nothin' to do with that Windy Hollow business. An' I'll make out, Edie ... leastways I'm gonna try ... my best. Edie? There's still time, Edie. What do you say, Edie?'

The crowd listened attentively, silent and curious. Their eyes went from Stacey to his wife and back again. When Stacey finished speaking all eyes turned to Edie. There was a pause, a sudden stillness, then Edie Stacey shook her head roughly, negatively, and shoving people aside, ran back towards the house, turning her back on her husband.

Stacey shrugged, his head sank noticeably lower and he turned and mounted. He took up the lead reins of the spare horse and the pack animal. Still he seemed loath to leave. He neck-reined the bay round, pointing its head towards the exit to the canyon. The two following horses fell into line and he touched his mount with his spurs. The little cavalcade began a slow trudge away from the town.

'Say, mister! Mister Stacey!' A thin, shrill voice cried out. 'Hold on a minute willya, Mister Stacey?'

Stacey reined in and glanced back in surprise. The crowd stared around them, trying to trace this sudden interruption. A small, slight figure stood alone, on the side where the crowd weren't collected. It was Annie Slocum. She was dressed in what were, although shabby enough, her best clothes, and she held an old, shabby carpet bag in one hand. She looked skinny and scared but determined, as though she had screwed up all her meagre courage for this brief moment. She hesitated momentarily when Stacey halted and looked round.

'I'll come with ya, Mister Stacey – Dave – if you want.' The voice was high-pitched with apprehension.

'You, Annie? Why. ...' Stacey held his horse in, nonplussed, confused. 'I'm goin' a long way, Annie. An' I ain't nothin' to you, I mean I ain't kin to you. ... Ain't no way of knowin' how things are gonna go with me. You'd be ... crazy ... to. ... I mean, where I'm goin', Annie ... an' how. There ain't no way of knowin'. ...'

'I'll come, jus' the same, if you'll take me.' The little skinny figure stood defiantly in the dirt road, carpet bag in hand, the young voice straining the warm air brittle with tension. 'I ain't got nothin' to stay here for. An' I don' want to stay with folks that don' want me. Folks that don' care a good goddam about me!' The thin voice cracked and threatened to break under the strain of strong emotion. 'Ain't gonna stay with folks that. ...' The voice broke, the head, previously held defiantly high, sank on to her chest and she broke down, weeping noisily. For a moment she remained like this, only a moment, then she raised her tear-stained face and looked right at Stacey. 'Aw, take me with you, Mister Stacey!' she pleaded openly. 'I can cook ... an' I won't complain none. Take me with you. Please!'

The crowd watched, dumbfounded, frozen into immobility. Stacey hesitated a moment – only a moment, undecided – then he nodded towards the spare saddled horse. 'Awright then, Annie. If you're sure. You're right welcome to come along. An' I give you my word, I'll keep my end of the bargain. Come on, mount up.'

The little figure scurried to the horses. She had a difficult job mounting. Finally Stacey took her carpet bag until she got into the saddle, her skirts awkwardly spread over the horse's back, but once she got settled she demanded the bag back as though it was extremely important to her. She sat awkwardly in the saddle, the bag clutched in one hand, the other hand on the saddle horn, and nodded to Stacey. 'Let's go Mister Stacey – Dave,' she said, and tried to smile.

Stacey nodded, looked back towards the crowd, waved to one or two faces – Caleb Grieve, Joe Gregory, Bea Gunther, Isaac Stone – then touched his spurs to his horse. The little cavalcade surged into motion again, the steel-shod hoofs scraping on the hard earth, and it moved away towards the canyon exit.

The little crowd watched it all the way, unable to take their eyes off the retreating backs. Soon the horses and their riders were out of sight.

THIRTEEN

The days – and the weeks – passed. Autumn turned gradually to early winter while Stacey and Annie Slocum made their way westwards. It was slow going. The girl was not good on a horse, though she tried her best, and this fact, coupled with Stacey's wounded arm, slowed them up noticeably. They were forced to make camp early each evening and sometimes had to stay in one place for a couple of days while they both recovered. Stacey worried continuously over this, although he took some reassurance from the fact that nobody had come up with them yet.

They were in just such a situation one morning when the cold woke up Stacey earlier than usual. He looked around the camp where they had been resting for three days. There was no sign of Annie.

Probably gone out after the pack horse, he thought. Critter musta bust his hobbles during the night. It had happened before. Have to make some new hobbles, he thought. Otherwise we'll lose the animal one of these days.

He looked around from where he lay in his

blankets, taking in the tidy, comfortable order of the camp. She sure is a handy woman, he reflected. If she can do this with a camp on the trail, what couldn't she do with a home? His mind went back to his life with Edie. It hadn't been like this then. Edie had hated domestic chores and their cabin had been permanently untidy. She'd disliked cooking too, and he could remember only messy, scrappy meals and little enjoyment of food. Now Annie, well, she seemed to love fixing his food and enjoyed good chow herself. Stacey, despite his worry, began to feel the growth of a kind of comfort he had never known before. If only they could move faster! If they could get over the Rockies before the winter set in! If only they could shake off Krieg!

He climbed out of his blankets. Annie would come back with the pack horse, soon. Meantime he could fetch water and get the fire going. They'd both be ready for breakfast.

He picked up their biggest pan and set off in the direction of the creek, clumping through the trees that surrounded their camp in the clearing. The water in the creek was cold but despite this he undressed and plunged briefly in: outdoor bathing wouldn't be possible soon; best make the most of it. He emerged puffing and blowing and shaking off water like a dog. Dried and clothed again, he took up the tin pan and walked up the creek to a point above where he had bathed. He dipped the pan in the creek and brought it out brim-full. It was as he straightened up that he heard the voice. 'Stay right where you are, Mister Stacey. Don't even think about movin'.'

Stacey jumped with fright, slopping water out of the pan, then froze. For a minute he remained motionless then slowly, steadily, straightened up.

'Don't move, I said!' The voice was urgent, threatening. 'Jus' stand still.'

In spite of the command, Stacey continued to straighten up and he even turned round. A lean, slightly stooped man was pointing a rifle at him. He obviously had advanced from the cover of the trees. 'You try anythin' an' I'll shoot ya,' he said. His grey face was set like concrete; his voice a slurred, close-mouthed threat.

'Krieg?' asked Stacey.

'Krieg.' The rifle was rock steady; the finger white on the trigger.

'I thought there was two of ya.' Stacey's voice was quiet, apathetic.

'Was. One quit. Only needs one.' The voice was cold, matter of fact. 'I'm takin' you back.'

Stacey gently shook his head. 'Naw,' he said. 'Naw, you ain't.' His voice was surprisingly calm. 'I ain't goin'. No way. Not with you nor nobody else, I ain't. Jus' ain't.'

Krieg sneered openly. 'You're going back, mister. If you don't go back alive you'll go back dead – an' don't think I don't mean it.'

'I believe you.' Stacey nodded slowly. He stood still, the pan of water still in his hand. 'An' you'd better believe me: I ain't goin' back, not alive, anyways. If I go back there I'm dead: might as well die here, where I'm clean, an' free.' He shrugged his shoulders. 'Where I've been happy,' he added. 'So if you're gonna shot me you'd better do it.'

'An' I will,' warned Krieg, the rifle held unwavering.

Stacey nodded in quiet resignation then deliberately began to walk back in the direction of their camp.

'Stay where you are mister!' cried Krieg. 'I won't tell you again.'

Stacey didn't even look round but kept on walking, as though Krieg simply wasn't there.

There were two violent explosions, so close together that they sounded like one. Stacey jerked, arching his back, dropping the tin pan and tumbling to the ground. Krieg thrust the lever of his Winchester down but held it in the down position. So he stood for a few seconds then he started towards Stacey. His steps were heavy, awkward, and as he went forward his pace increased until it was a staggering run. He stumbled past Stacey, sinking as he ran, and collapsed in a heap on the dew-moist earth.

For a minute there was no movement and only the noise of birds startled by the explosions, then Stacey stirred in the grass. He dragged himself to his feet, shaking and white-faced. He began to examine himself all over – his belly, his chest, his back, his legs.

There were no holes in him. He couldn't believe it. He searched again, certain that he must have been shot. But there was no blood, no pain, no inability to move. He shook his head in wonder, his hands still wandering over his body in unbelieving search of wounds. Slowly, dazed, he looked around him: trees ... grass ... Annie Slocum holding a rifle ... two horses grazing close by, as though nothing had happened.

It took him several minutes to come to his senses. Then he walked towards the spot where Krieg lay, face down, on the ground. He was silent and unmoving. Stacey turned him over. Blood soaked his shirt and vest front, indicating a bullet exit wound in his chest or belly. He was already dead.

Stacey turned and made his way to Annie. She was sitting on the damp earth, her head held in her hands. The rifle lay on the ground where she had dropped it.

'Was it you?' Stacey asked, realizing as he said it, the foolishness of his question.

Annie looked up. Her face was white as chalk. Her lips moved but no words came out for several seconds, then, 'He was goin' to shoot you,' she said.

Stacey nodded. 'Yeah. You're right. He was. Another minute an' I'da been dead.' He stood there, unable to think, to act. 'Was you out lookin' for the stray horse?'

She nodded. 'Was on my way back with him when I saw *him*.' Her voice was almost inaudible. She nodded towards Krieg. 'I guessed who he was, an' followed him. He was goin' to shoot you,' she said again. 'He was. I know it.'

Stacey nodded again. He could not find words, did not know what to say. Eventually he said lamely, 'I didn't know you could use a rifle.'

'I can't. I just' pointed it at him an' pulled the trigger. Lord forgive me.' She burst into uncontrollable weeping.

Stacey took a deep breath. 'Well, if it hadn't happened to him it woulda happened to me,' he told her. 'So I ain't complainin'. Seems to me he got some of his own kinda justice.' He put an arm round the weeping girl's shoulders. 'Come on, Annie,' he said. 'Time we got outa here.'

The storekeeper at Fort Walla Walla put the coffee and sugar on the counter. Two sides of bacon, two sacks of flour and a sack of beans stood by the doorway, ready for lifting on to the pack horse. 'You cut it mighty fine.' He shook his head in mild disapproval. 'Jus' got across the Rockies in time. Few days more an' it'da been too late.' He glanced at the snow falling softly and steadily outside. 'Ain't safe to cut it that fine. You got no idea the kind of things that can happen to folks stranded out there in the winter.'

'We didn' have no choice,' said Stacey simply.

'Yeah, well, I guess there's some like that,' nodded the storekeeper. 'But they ain't all as lucky as you.'

'That's a fact.' Stacey grinned at Annie. 'We sure are lucky.'

'You know where you're gonna be stayin'?' The storekeeper's eyes went again to the falling snow outside the window.

'No. No idea, yet.' The customer didn't seem to be too concerned.

'Well, there's a three-quarter-built cabin, 'bout two miles down the trail from here. You can see it from the trail. Close by a big boulder with a tree growin' right out of it. You can't miss it. Fella was buildin' it jus' before last winter, but he changed his mind and went back east. Can be a hard life out here, for a man on his own.'

'Nobody mind if we stayed there a while? Through the winter?' The idea was a welcome one to Stacey. Annie's eyes too had begun to shine.

'No. Nobody would min'. You'd be awright there, too. Get a deer now an' then. Elk too, maybe. Fish too – salmon – 'cause you ain't far from the river. 'Course you'd have to put a bit of work in, make it habitable, 'fore the winter really sets in. But there's plenty timber around – for buildin' an' for firewood. You won't go hungry or cold in the winter, long as you're prepared to work.' He nodded towards their supplies. 'You want a hand to load this stuff?'

They did see it from the trail, three-quarters built, as the man had said, right down to the glassless window covered with a stiff, flapping hide.

It was only half-roofed but inside, the part under the half-roof was mostly dry. A rough stone fireplace with a chimney occupied one wall. 'There's hewn logs outside,' said Stacey. 'We can use them. Won't take me long to complete the roof. That's all we need for now. Rest can wait till spring comes.'

'An' we can live here, while you're doin' it,'

added Annie. 'Right here, under the bit of roof that is there. We'll keep a good fire in that fireplace. Be right comfortable.' She threw a mischievous look at him. 'Be warm too, you an' me … right warm at times.'

Stacey reached out and drew her to him. 'I didn' ever say.' He spoke quietly, over his shoulder, into her ear. 'But, well, with bein' on the trail with you … an' all that … I've grown mighty fond of you, Annie.'

'Is that a fact?' Her body moulded itself against his and her voice was warm, soft. 'An' what do you think we oughta do about that?' Her body pressed even closer to him.

'Well,' He wasn't good with words. He stumbled awkwardly. 'I mean … that is … if you're willin'. …' He stopped in confusion.

She squirmed against him. 'Oh, I am,' she murmured. 'I surely am. Now you unsaddle them horses outside an' I'll get a fire roarin' in that fireplace. I can think of better things to do than stan' aroun' here watchin' the snow.'